THE GIFT OF SUNDERLAND

J.E. Rogers

Illustrated by, Guy Atherfold

MW01074320

This is a fictional work. The names, characters, and incidents are solely the concepts and products of the author's imagination or are used to create a fictitious story and should not be construed as real.

The Gift of Sunderland:

ISBN 10: 0-990751201

ISBN 13: 978-0-9907512-0-5

Copyright © 2014 Jeanne E. Rogers

Published by Acadia Publishing Group, LLC

All rights reserved. No part of this book may be used or reproduced in any manner whatsoever without written permission, except in the case of brief quotations, reviews and articles.

Cover Design: Guy Atherfold
Illustrations: Guy Atherfold
www.guyatherfold.com
Book formatting: Erika M Szabo
www.authorerikamszabo.com

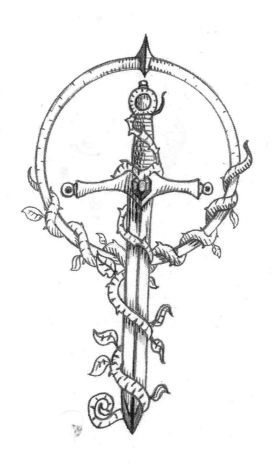

THE GIFT OF SUNDERLAND

An Australian Fantasy Adventure
By, J.E. Rogers
Illustrated by, Guy Atherfold
ACADIA PUBLISHING GROUP, LLC

Dedication

To

Lorri Gallo Rowe

With all my Love and Gratitude

CONTENTS

PRAISE
for *THE SWORD OF DEMELZA*

MOONBEAM CHILDREN'S BOOK AWARDS – GOLD MEDAL WINNER

WRITER'S DIGEST
Winner! Honorable Mention–2013 eBook Awards
"Beyond excellent, from the terrific illustrations on the cover and throughout the book, so well-placed by the author to convey the characters' depth in plot."

Judge, Writer's Digest eBook Awards 2013

READER'S FAVORITE INT'L BOOK AWARDS – BRONZE MEDAL WINNER
"I hope there will be a sequel as the characters brought to life...are well worth following in their future adventures. *The Sword of Demelza* is great fantasy, and I highly recommend it."

Reader's Favorite Reviewer

BOOK OF THE YEAR FINALIST – ForeWord Reviews
"Told in crisp, page-turning prose, readers of all ages will find this to be an engaging novel built around a framework of moral guidance."

PUBLISHERS WEEKLY – "In this entertaining debut, Rogers uses her love of Australian wildlife to deliver a rousing Redwallesque fantasy, in which a coalition of creatures embarks on an epic quest."

BENJAMIN FRANKLIN DIGITAL GOLD HONOREE!
"There are a number of books with anthropomorphized animals, but there is no other book quite like this one. The Sword of Demelza is unlike any anthropomorphized animal story on the market today."

AUTHOR'S NOTE

Dear Readers,

First, I would like to thank those of you who have read, *The Sword of Demelza*, and now have chosen to read, *The Gift of Sunderland*. Welcome back to Sunderland. I hope you enjoy the adventure!

Secondly, I want to thank my editors, Gavin Doyle, for his instruction, his advice, and his continual support, and Beth Bruno, for her expertise. I also want to mention, Margot Finke, my friend and a wonderful children's author and book editor, for her suggestions and advice. Somehow, the Universe has guided me to these people, and I am forever grateful.

To all of those who I begged to read *The Gift of Sunderland*, I sincerely thank you. You are too many to mention, but you know who you are. I want to especially thank two of my young readers, Dylan Jones, and Erika-Elizabeth Caswell, both ten years of age. You are wonderful.

Last, and certainly not least, I must thank Guy Atherfold, for the beautiful illustrations he created. He brought my characters to life and inspired me. Thank you, sir. I have no words.

One of the major reasons for writing these adventures is to introduce young and old alike to the unusual flora and fauna of Australia. There are more unusual animals in OZ than any other place on the planet. Sadly, many of them are endangered. I have provided a glossary at the back of the book. It will give you some information about the animals that roam Sunderland, and there are links there for you. If you like, you can read more about the animals in our story, just follow the links.

There are endangered animals all over the globe. Habitat destruction by humans is one of the major threats to their survival. Somehow we must learn how to live in harmony with our fellow creatures. After all, we share this earth and are intrinsically connected with them.

Sincerely,

Jeanne E. Rogers

Danbury, February 2015

P.S. If you have any questions, or simply want to chat, feel free to contact me!

www.facebook.com/australianfantasyadventures

www.warriorechidna.blogspot.com

www.pinterest.com/warriorechidna

www.twitter.com/warriorechidna

Jeanne.rogers22@gmail.com

CAST OF ANIMAL CHARACTERS

The Glossary at the back of the book will provide information on each of the following animals and much more.

Waylond Ayers	Numbat
Morlund Ayers	Numbat
Roland Ayers	Numbat
Fergal	Quoll
Wulfgar	Stoat
Bunyip	Stoat
Wilbing	Kookaburra
Simkin	Bilby
Nedra	Tasmanian Devil
Flitch	Thylacine
Bede	Bilby
Rufus	Dibbler
Monti & Jiemba	Tasmanian Devils

Also:

Chloe	Wood Nymph of the Styx
The Forest as itself	

PROLOGUE

Waylond Ayers stood on the banks of the Gabbling. The water of the river rushed by forming eddies around smooth rocks. Acadia and Demelza, territories within the realm of Sunderland, teemed with life, but today the Forest was quiet. Warm breezes blew through the trees and ruffled Waylond's fur. A green leaf drifted down before him and dropped into the river. The current pulled it under. The leaf rose briefly to the surface, then disappeared beneath the dark water.

Waylond scanned the woods on the far side of the Gabbling. Not another soul was in sight, and he was grateful for the solitude. He had not been to this embankment since the tragedy. The memory of what had happened at this spot on the river was clear in his mind, and it stung his heart like the poisonous bite of a brown snake. He bent a knee to the hard earth and thought about all that had passed between himself and his brother, Morlund. Then, slipping his claw beneath the gold clasp that held his cape around his neck, he released it and let the cloak fall to the ground.

A royal numbat, his family was composed of an ancestry of mighty marsupials, sworn to care for and protect the weaker inhabitants of the countryside. They made sure the cycle of life and death continued as the Forest intended, and maintained peace and harmony among all creatures. As in times gone by, Guardianship was passed down. The voices of the Forest's former Guardians spoke the name of the next in line. He was

1

chosen and would need to take on the obligations expected of him.

But those heavy responsibilities could not hold him in the present. Dark memories clouded his thoughts as the mighty marsupial squeezed his eyes shut. The breeze skittered across the river bringing painful recollections with it. Rising from the chattering waters, his memories arrived on the whistling wind.

"Waylond!" The boy's shrill voice called out as he ran along the dirt path toward the river. "I'll beat you there!" Leaving their mother behind to set up a picnic lunch, they hurried on toward the Gabbling. Waylond caught up to his older brother, Morlund, and tackled him. They rolled together in the tall weeds, giggling and nipping playfully at each other.

"Careful, boys," their mother's voice warned from within the trees. "Don't get too close to the river. Stay near."

Rising to their feet, both boys ignored their mother's warning and headed closer to the rushing water. They played near the edge of the river and wandered too close to the Gabbling's slick banks.

It happened in the blink of an eye. The riverbank seemed to reach out and take hold of Morlund's feet, and he fell into the river. Waylond thrust out a paw, but he could not reach his brother in time.

Waylond screamed for help, and their mother sprinted to the spot. She raced down along the bank until she was close to her son. Jumping into the river, the current pulled her under.

Rising to the surface, she clutched at Morlund, and gasped for air. Waylond watched helplessly as his mother shoved and pushed Morlund toward the bank. Finally, she lifted Morlund and dropped him in a heap onto a flat boulder. She tried to hold on to the smooth surface, but she was exhausted. Her paw slid off the edge and the swift current embraced her and carried her away.

"Mother," Waylond shouted from the shore. "Mother!" He ran along the river, keeping her in sight for as long as he could. He lifted his paw, asking the Forest for help, trying to use his immature sorcery, but he couldn't. A swift wind whistled through the treetops in response to his call. He stopped. He stood staring, his chest heaving. He no longer saw her head above the rolling water.

"Mother!" Waylond woke from his reverie. He was alone again on the bank of the river, staring out at the flat rock—the rock that had saved his brother. It was the same rock his mother could not hold on to. Sadness gripped him and he scolded himself, as he had done so many times before, for not being able to save her.

Waylond alongside the Gabbling River

Chapter 1

As evening fell, Waylond stood before the ancient gum tree and contemplated his home. The tree had fallen so long ago that the event was no longer a part of the Forest's memory, but the dwelling that had been carved out of it was home. *It's a comfortable home*, he thought. *Usually*. Waylond's family history was a source of pride to his father, Roland Ayers, patriarch, advisor to his extended family and Guardian of the Forest. The creatures throughout Sunderland recognized his strength and the power of his sorcery, sorcery all the Ayers possessed. Now there was unrest within this comfortable home, and Roland Ayers would have to stand firm. Verdigris, the collective voice of Guardians past, had spoken and the Forest delivered its message. The name of the next Guardian had been announced to Roland. No one questioned Verdigris, and no one questioned the appointment. The decision would be obeyed. Waylond's father was dedicated to the Forest, and the conflict within his family would not shake him.

Yes, the old home is comfortable, Waylond thought as he walked toward the front door. *Many pleasant memories dwell within those bark walls*. A light shone in his father's library window, and he saw his brother pacing back and forth before it. *It must be another argument.* As Waylond entered the home, Morlund was on his way out and caught him by the arm.

"Morlund, don't start again," Waylond said, yanking his arm free from his brother's grasp. "The decision has been made, and we simply need to accept it."

"I don't have to," Morlund said, jabbing a claw, nearly touching Waylond's nose. "You should have declined."

"You know we don't control this," Waylond said patiently. "I can't decline."

Waylond walked past his brother and headed for the library where he was certain to find his father. He had tried to talk to his brother many times. They had argued the matter over and over again, but it made no sense to quarrel. He knew the responsibility was his even though his heart was filled with doubt. His responsibilities as blacksmith to the local inhabitants would have to come to an end, as new and more important responsibilities would have to be acknowledged.

Waylond found his father sitting at his oak desk. Steam curled into the air from the hot cup of tea beside his paw. He had fond memories of the library. When he and his brother were young they would sit for hours and read while their father worked, but those days were gone. The shelves were crowded with dusty books handed down through generations. Waylond scanned some of the volumes and read the titles on the spines: *Forest Potions, Cures for Wombats, Healthy Foods for Dibblers and Seasonal Allergies of the Wallaby* were just a few of the leather-bound books. Some volumes contained histories of the lives of their ancestors, while others described the powers of the Forest. One in particular, *The Book of Memory*, was bound in red leather, its edges gilded in gold. It was open on the desk, and Roland ran his paw across the pages as he read. He referred to the book when he had a problem or needed a medicine for various ailments that might befall the Forest's creatures.

Roland looked up and smiled. "Ah, my son. How are you this evening?"

"I'm fine, Father, except..." Waylond hesitated. A book on the top shelf caught his eye. It stuck out from the rest, and he reached up and took the book down to examine it. "I've never seen this volume before, Father." He thumbed through a few of the pages. "I thought thylacines no longer roamed the forest." He scratched an ear and ran a paw over the black stripe that stretched from his pointy nose and over his eyes. The dark stripe signaled his maturity.

"Thylacines do indeed roam the forests," Roland said. "They wander the dark wood of Sunderland." Roland leaned back in his chair, rested his paw on its arm and peeked over his reading spectacles at Waylond. "They are a fierce, but lonely creature..." His voice trailed off. He cleared his throat. "Now, what about you? You look concerned. Talk to me."

Waylond replaced the book on the shelf and turned to his father. "It's Morlund. I can't stand the arguments. He can't accept the decision."

"Ah, yes. I thought that might be the problem." Roland picked up his cup of tea and took a sip. "Sit, Waylond," he said with a smile, pointing to a chair next to his desk.

Waylond strode across the room, grabbed the chair, and pulled it closer to his father. Placing his teacup on its saucer, Roland looked out the window. The evening was warm, and night was closing in. "It's getting late," he muttered under his breath.

He sighed and looked back at Waylond. "Soon you will take up the mantle of the Guardian. This book and all it contains will be given to you." He reached up and removed his reading glasses, setting them beside the book. "You'll need to carry on its traditions. You'll need to use its contents for the good of Acadia and all of Sunderland. Above all, you'll need to be strong."

"I know, Father. I've read it so many times that I know every word, prayer and potion by heart. I've committed every cure to memory." He placed his paw on the desk and studied his father's face. "I am strong, Father. Your belief in me has made me so, but—"

Roland raised a paw, stopping his son. "There is no room for discussion, Waylond. Your name has been whispered in the wind of the Forest. The voice of Verdigris has spoken. You are to be the next Guardian."

"Morlund does not see it the same way. He is bitter and angry. He blames me for what happened..." He leaned toward his father. "I cannot change the past," he said. "I am doing my best to keep my temper..." He ran a paw through the fur on his head, as a low growl rumbled in his throat.

"What happened is in the past. It was an accident," Roland said. Waylond recognized a touch of sadness in his father's

8

voice. "Your brother can be…he is a strong willed numbat. Suffice it to say he was not chosen." He pointed a claw at Waylond. "*You* have been chosen." He let out a heavy sigh. "I am growing old, Waylond. I am not as strong as I once was." He stood, closed the book and lifted it slowly from his desk. Embracing it, he looked down at his son. "You must accept this responsibility, Waylond. Do not let your brother's anger hold you back." The lamplight flickered in his eyes, as a determined look came upon his face. "It's not enough for me to believe in you. You must believe in yourself. I know you have questions and concerns." Still holding the book, Roland placed a paw lightly on his son's shoulder. "There are no mistakes," he said calmly. "The voices of Guardians past see a greatness in you, as I do. You have the strength and wisdom of a true Guardian."

The sound of footsteps in the hallway outside the library took their attention. The door opened with a crash. The bookshelves shook and volumes dropped to the floor as Morlund stepped in.

"I want to hear it straight from you, Father, here and now, in front of my brother," Morlund said. "Tell me why this…this *weakling* has been chosen." His paws balled into fists.

"We've just discussed this," Roland said sternly. He placed the book on his desk and walked around it to face Morlund. "There is nothing more to talk about."

"Yes, there is!" Morlund said with a snarl. "Waylond is not worthy enough to take on the responsibilities of Guardian, let alone the power of the sword. And *you*, Father, you are afraid to forge the sword! Why is it that all we do is cure some miserable wombat down by the river? We are more powerful than that. We should take up that power and use it. After all, aren't we the Great Ayers family?" he shouted. "Aren't we meant to become the great Guardians we are destined to be?"

"Yes, you are right, we are the Ayers of Sunderland, and we will carry on the traditions of the Guardians as generations before us have. We use our powers for the good of the Forest and the creatures that live here, not for our own gain. You know that, Morlund. " Roland scowled at him. "And the sword… The sword is to be forged by the Guardian. No other creature can create it no matter how hard they try. It is a final symbol of the Guardian and his acceptance of his responsibilities. The powers it contains are nothing until the Guardian has accepted it. Once it is joined with the crystal, Guardianship is complete, but it can only be completed in its proper time. If it is created too soon and falls into the wrong paws, its powers will be corrupted. You know that. Waylond knows that." Roland took a step closer to Morlund. "Why do you continue to question me? Why do we continue to have this conversation?"

"Morlund…" Waylond said, moving toward his brother.

"I am through with you, Waylond!" Morlund removed his dagger from its sheath.

"Do not do anything that you will regret, Morlund," Waylond said, offering his paw to his brother.

"I don't want to hear what you have to say," Morlund snapped. "You're a coward, not worthy. You wouldn't know how to handle the sword even if father forged it!"

"Put that knife away," Roland barked. "We are family. We will not allow such discord to control us."

"We would have been if it weren't for him." Morlund glared at his brother.

"I am the head of this family," Roland said, pounding a fist on his desk. "You are defying everything we stand for as Ayers." He raised his arm and pointed a claw at his son. "The *Forest* will know, Morlund."

"I am sick of your foolish philosophies and lectures, Father," Morlund snarled. "You can't threaten me. Once I have the sword, I will control its power." He narrowed his gaze toward his brother and charged, his dagger held before him.

Waylond moved forward to meet Morlund, but Roland stepped between the two. Thrusting the dagger with all his might, Morlund struck. Roland looked at the dagger in Morlund's paw and placed his own paw on the wound in his chest. "Morlund, my son." He slumped to the floor.

"What have you done?" Waylond yelled. For a moment he felt his gut twist into knots of pain. His heart was beating so fast that it took his breath away. Then the anger came, flowing up from inside, rising like lava, his rage ready to erupt. He slowly gazed at Morlund, who stood over his father, the dagger in his paw, his father's blood dripping to the floor.

"He shouldn't have interfered," Morlund said, shaking his head. "This wouldn't have happened if you'd admit you were not up to the task." He looked down at his father, then to the dagger in his paw. He released it and it dropped to the ground. "We are the Great Ayers of Sunderland." He scanned the library. Years of the Forest's history and Ayers' lineage surrounded them. Waylond saw anguish and anger on his brother's face. "We should have more than this ancient tree and its books!" he sobbed, tears glistening in his eyes. "We should have more than reverence from the lowly creatures that live in the forest."

With all his fury, Waylond lunged at Morlund and threw him against the shelves. The two brothers fell to the floor and rolled over each other, grasping, clawing and biting. Morlund reached out and grabbed his brother by the throat, choking and shaking him. Waylond brought his arm around, striking the side of Morlund's head with his fist. Then he took him by the scruff of his neck, pulled him to his feet and pressed him against the bookshelves. He held him there with his forearm pushed against his throat.

"Get out of here," Waylond hissed into his brother's face. "Get out and never come back!" Waylond shoved his brother toward the door of the library.

Morlund stumbled and reached for the doorframe. "You think this is over," he bellowed. "It's not over, Waylond!" He spat out his brother's name as though it were poison on his tongue. "You know in your heart that you are not worthy. Our mother would agree if you hadn't killed her." Turning, he limped down the hallway and slammed the front door as he left.

Bowing his head, Waylond dropped to his knees. "Father," he whispered. Roland's eyes fluttered open as Waylond lifted him gently into his arms.

"Waylond."

"I'm here, Father."

"You must not allow this to alter your course." Roland raised a paw to touch his son's arm, his words sputtering out between breaths. "Go to Verden Glen. There you will find the crystal. Forge the sword in its time. Answer the call of the Forest. Believe in yourself." His eyes closed, and he was gone.

Waylond stood in front of his home and watched a cloak of mist floating on the cool morning air. The fallen tree was once a place for family and happiness. Now it was nothing more than ancient wood. Tightening his cape against the chill, he searched the windows. They were dark like his thoughts. He hesitated a moment, then lifted his paw. With his palm facing the ancient home, he closed his eyes and called on the powers of the Forest. A spark ignited and the ancient tree burst into flames. "Forgive me."

Watching the inferno, he thought about the burning books within. Now that his father was gone, he was the Guardian. He would take up the mantle and forge the sword, but he needed time. This chapter in his life had come to an end. What had happened here weighed heavy on his heart and he could not face his responsibility just yet. As he turned to walk away, he sent a silent prayer to the Forest, asking for strength.

Chapter 2

It was close to sundown when Waylond arrived at Verden Glen deep in the Forest of Acadia. He approached the Glen, slowed his pace, and scanned the surrounding wood. He knew the portal was there, part of the thick wall of shrubbery and dense undergrowth that stood before him. A kookaburra's maniacal laugh pierced the Forest's trees. Waylond narrowed his gaze and looked up. Every branch and bough vibrated over his head. Searching the foliage, he tried to locate the bird.

Again he studied the foliage, and lifting his paw, closed his eyes. With his palm facing the greenery, he whispered to the surrounding Forest. The dry leaves at his feet began to move. A circle of air wrapped around his legs and rose in waves up his brown leather boots to his knees. The hem of his green cape rippled with the movement, and the gold trim at its edge began to glow. Sparkling, the radiance sent a cascade of light pouring to the ground, where it gathered for a moment before soaking into the earth. The air continued to rise, circling at his waist, then it climbed slowly to his neck and head.

I can do this. Waylond opened his eyes. *Verdigris spoke with certainty. I must complete the sword in its time and become the new*

Guardian. I must take my father's place. A single tear rolled from his eye down to the tip of his pointy snout and fell to the ground at his feet. He slowly lifted his head, and the portal shimmered before him. The opening was alight with green flames that rose from the ground and twisted to the treetops. Beyond the portal, he could see the wooden altar at the base of the giant tingle tree. This was a place of meditation for the Guardians, a place of communion with the Forest. He would find the green crystal, as his father instructed, beneath the altar.

He passed through the doorway and walked in. The flaming entrance closed behind him with a hiss of extinguished flames. Dropping respectfully to his knees, he cast his paw beneath the altar searching for the hidden compartment he knew would be there. Finally, his claw touched the latch, and with a click a heart-shaped door opened. The cache was empty. The cackle of the Kookaburra splintered the air, and he realized he was not alone. A humming in the treetops floated down to him, and he ran a paw over one ear.

"I feel your presence, brother," Waylond said, rising to his feet. "Show yourself."

Morlund appeared from a dark crevice in the roots of the tingle tree. A black cape draped from his shoulders, and the tops of his black boots ended at his knees. In his right paw, he carried a halberd made of the finest steel from the mines of Mt. Olga. In his left paw, he held a green faceted crystal, which he tossed idly into the air and back into his open paw. The axe-blade of the weapon rose over his head, its steel edge directed at

Waylond. The spear at the top of the weapon pointed to the darkening sky.

"Brother," Waylond said, "have you forgotten what Father taught us? His wishes? His instructions?" He stared deeply into Morlund's yellow eyes. He found nothing there but contempt and anger.

"No, Waylond. I have not forgotten," Morlund said. "You are the one with the short memory. Have you forgotten who we are?" Morlund took a step toward Waylond, a grin forming on his face. "You and I were always so different. I was the strong one, the oldest. You spent most of your youth sniveling at Father's feet. And Mother, well, I don't want to bring up that memory."

"I have forgiven you for what you did to Father," Waylond said. "Those who are weak cannot forgive. Forgiveness is a virtue of the strong, Brother." He held out his paw to Morlund. "I know that Mother saved you from the raging river. My memories of her are filled with love. Your memory of the accident has filled you with anger and bitterness." He pointed to the crystal. "I won't let you take the crystal from this place."
Morlund widened his stance and pointed the halberd directly at his brother. "And you won't stop me." He dropped the crystal into a leather pouch that hung around his neck. "Let's see if you can take it away."

Waylond brushed dry dirt from his paws and snatched up a large leafless tree limb. Holding it in front of his chest, he prepared for Morlund's first move. Morlund swung the halberd effortlessly, as he took one deliberate step toward his brother.

Morlund at Verden Glen

The weapon sliced the air, and Waylond ducked out of the way as the great axe whizzed by his ear. Waylond lifted the wooden branch, connecting with the haft of the halberd as it veered toward him again. The force of their weapons coming together threw Waylond backward. With his feet flying off the ground, Waylond landed hard against a nearby tree.

The leaves above Waylond's head vibrated, as the halberd cut through the air again, missing him by inches. He rose to his feet once more, and thrust the branch toward his brother, stopping the advance of Morlund's weapon. Twisting to avoid another direct hit, Waylond stumbled and fell back against the tree once more, hitting his head. The impact cut a gash beneath his ear, and blood trickled down his fur to his neck. Still, he held tightly to his wooden weapon.

Morlund moved toward his brother, his halberd looming overhead. As the weapon dropped toward him, Waylond rose to his feet and thrust a powerful paw up, meeting the shaft midway just below the axe head. The two brothers now stood face to face in a contest of wills, each gripping the halberd.

Groaning under the effort, Waylond swung the wooden branch at his brother's head. But Morlund ducked, and the branch grazed his ear. In one swift movement, Morlund wrenched the halberd from Waylond and took the wooden weapon from his paw. Careening backward, Waylond fell to the ground. With the wind knocked out of him, he looked up at Morlund, who flung the wooden branch to the dirt beside him, and lowered the spear point of his halberd to Waylond's nose.

"I should kill you," Morlund snarled. "But I won't. I want to be there when you recognize the power we can have if we stand together. With the sword we can control the Forest." Morlund bent over his brother. "Don't you see that?"

Waylond shook his head in an effort to clear it. A terrible sadness gripped him, and he could not lift himself from the ground. Contorting in pain, he looked up at his brother. "There will come a time, Morlund, when we will both regret this moment. We will both recognize our place in the Forest."

"Let's hope it's sooner than later!" Morlund said. "I will wait for you to come to your senses."

The cackle of the kookaburra filled the air as a stiff wind blew through the canopy. The trunks of the nearby tingle trees cracked open and green flames surrounded the brothers. Together they watched, as the branch Waylond had used for a weapon, sank into the ground and then slowly re-emerged. It had become a smooth staff; its flaws had disappeared and were replaced with glowing runes. Now it was a true weapon, a gift from the Forest. Waylond took hold of the staff and slowly rose to his feet. "We will answer to the Forest, Morlund."

Morlund took a step backward and nodded. The wall surrounding Verden Glen shimmered and the flaming door opened. "Next time, Waylond," Morlund said, "the Forest will serve me." Turning, he walked through the portal and disappeared into the woods, his massive halberd resting easily on his shoulder, the green crystal still within the pouch around his neck.

Waylond dropped to his knees and looked up through the trees to the grey evening sky. One gasping breath filled his lungs, and he let out a roar of pain and despair. *Father, I have failed.*

Chapter 3

THREE YEARS LATER

Don't go near the Gabbling!

Fergal stood on the bank of the river and replayed her mother's warning in her head. The roaring river rushed through the old berry thicket near her home in Danby then continued its course, cutting through all of Sunderland. It was hard to ignore the river's roar as she stood on the Gabbling's banks and stared into its churning waters. This time of year, the river was swollen with spring's first melting snows from far away icy mountains. She didn't think anyone from down in Danby had ever been as far as the mountains in northern Sunderland. *Someday, maybe I'll see those mountains.* She heard her brothers' laughter and turned to look at them.

"Don't go near the Gabbling!" Their taunting grew louder, and when she glanced back, they giggled and rolled in the grass holding their bellies.

Fergal was the smallest of her family and the only girl of three rambunctious young quolls. She was half the size of her two brothers, and her spots weren't as white as theirs. Their brilliant spots stood out on their light brown fur like a white arum lily on a field of gold. Her colors were muted, dull. Mother said it was related to the season in which she was born, and that she would blossom in time. But Fergal knew it was only an excuse to make her feel better.

"Fergal! Fergal! Gurgle Gurgle! Don't go near the Gabbling." She met their taunts with a determined gaze. Still, she believed there was something in her, something special. She reached into the pocket of her overalls and wrapped her paw around the tiny acorn she always kept with her. She took it out to look at it. The acorn was a precious gift from her mother, who had painted an exquisite landscape of their home on the small seed. It was a reminder that all great things emerge from small beginnings. The slight weight of the acorn reminded her of her mother's faith and lent her confidence. Narrowing her eyes, she shouted, "I'm tired of you making fun of me. You better be quiet."

"Uh-oh," one brother squealed. "She's really mad now!" Their laughter began anew.

"You can't rock jump that river!" Her older brother shouted. "I can jump across using each stone as a step. You can't even reach the first one. Your legs are too short for that. You're tiny, your spots are dull, and so's your brain." One brother slapped the other on the back, urging him on.

She pushed her paw deep into her pocket and let the acorn fall safely in. Her lips curled into a snarl as she bent down to pick up a stone. Baring her sharp little teeth, she aimed it at her brothers.

With her eyes filled with tears and her vision blurring, Fergal pulled her arm back and prepared to throw the stone. She gasped with surprise when she slipped on the muddy bank and fell into the river. There was no time to scream.

In a flash, the swift current snatched her away from the riverbank. Try as she might, she could not grasp the rocks. Her claws sliced over their slick surface, smooth and quick, like her mother's knife sliced through peach pudding. The sound of the gurgling water filled her ears. Her heart raced and she blinked away the water that splashed into her eyes. The undercurrent grabbed her and carried her downstream.

She saw her brothers dash away. Their laughter turned to calls for help, but their voices faded as she rolled and tumbled with the foaming rapids. She thrashed and splashed, swallowing great gulps of water. Struggling to keep her head above the swirling currents, she continued to travel with the river far from her home. A strong surge of the current pushed her up and when she opened her eyes she noticed a small tree growing on the bank of the river. Its branches leaned out over the water. Like thin arms, they seemed to reach for her.

When she got closer, she kicked with fierce thrusts and shot out her paws to clamp them to the branch. Clutching the branch, she continued to kick fiercely with her hind legs. The

Fergal by the Gabbling

current fought her, trying to rip her paws from the tree and reclaim her. As she held on tightly, it seemed the tree's roots strained to hold on to the riverbank. The tree creaked and bent under Fergal's weight. And now, this scrawny tree was the only thing that stood between her and the rapids. Exhausted, she sucked in great gulps of air. *What a terrible end this is. Swallowed up by the Gabbling. The very thing Mama had warned me about.* She closed her eyes. Soon, she felt the muscles in her arms weaken. *How much longer can I hold on?*

The loose skin around her neck tightened as a paw gripped it and lifted her out of the cold water. Startled, she opened her eyes wide and let go of the branch. A full-grown numbat held her at arm's length, pulling her from the rapids. Brown boots and dark brown pants covered the large marsupial's long legs, and a three-button vest covered his chest. Intense black eyes stared into hers. His look was unsympathetic and stern, but Fergal held his gaze.

The numbat's brushy tail flicked and swished as Fergal studied him. The breeze ruffled his reddish brown fur and black stripes ran from the tip of his nose, over his eyes to his pointed ears. *He's a big one. I've never seen one so huge.*

"So, are you lost?" the numbat asked in a detached tone. His deep voice frightened Fergal, but she heard a hint of compassion and warmth in it.

"Uh, no. Not really," she said. Still hanging from the great paw in mid air, she tried to shake off the water that drenched her coat and pants.

"Humph. You look lost to me."

"That depends on what your definition of 'lost' is," Fergal said. "Uh, do ya think you could put me down? Preferably over there on the bank of the river," she said, pointing toward the shore. The water encircled the numbat's legs, but he stood firm, unmoved by it. Still holding Fergal at arm's length, he took two giant strides to shore and lowered her to the ground. Fergal shook head to foot. The green jacket and pants her mother had made were soaked and clung to her small furry frame. She shook again. Beads of water flew in every direction. She scrunched her shoulders to her ears and smiled sheepishly at the numbat.

"You still look lost to me," he said, staring down at her. "And, by the way, the fur on your head is standing up in spikes." He turned his back to Fergal and began to ramble up the hill into the woods. On his way he bent down and picked up a pail of water. He did not look back. He just kept walking.

"Lost? Spikes?" She ran a paw over her head to smooth down her fur. "I'm not lost. I meant to do that," Fergal yelled after him. "I was swimming!" She ran her paw across her snout to push away some of the water. "Hey! Wait a minute," Fergal shouted. "What... Hey! Ohhh..." Fergal took one last look upstream. "I have no idea how far from home I am," she said. "Should I try to find my way back on my own?"

Frustrated, Fergal stomped her foot to the ground and followed the numbat into the woods. She scrambled up a sharp incline, flicking low branches and shrubs out of her way as she went. At the top there stood a rustic shack made of timber, its back against a rocky mountain, its front open to the forest.

Flames from a blacksmith's forge burned in a brick furnace beneath its thatched roof, and an anvil was set alongside it on a large stump of an old tree. The great numbat lifted a small blade from the fire with a pair of tongs and placed it on the anvil. Grasping his hammer, he struck its edge steadily. Sparks flashed as bits of metal flew and buzzed off the blade.

"I see you're a blacksmith," Fergal said, as she stepped into the warmth of the numbat's hut. He looked up for just a second, then went back to his work. Fergal glanced toward the woods. The sun peeked out from behind the treetops. Its orange glow fell into the numbat's small forge. A ghost of a breeze swirled around her and she shivered. The sun would soon set, and Fergal was wet, weary and hungry.

"My name is Fergal."

The numbat stopped mid swing, and looked at Fergal, grunted once, and then lowered the hammer down with a crash.

"So, Fergal," he said, without looking up. "What brings you here?" He slammed the hammer down onto the dagger again.

"Well," Fergal said, giggling, "I guess the Gabbling did." She circled the small shed while looking at the various tools that hung from the walls. On one wall, in a dark corner, a sword hung, its point directed to the ground. The hilt appeared unfinished; a circular opening hinted that something was missing. Fergal stopped and considered it. *That looks heavy. I bet I wouldn't be able to hold that sword.* Next to the blade a dark blue hooded cape hung. It was made of velvet, with grey fur at the neck and gold trim at the bottom.

"Don't touch anything!" he warned her.

Taken aback by his sharp tone, Fergal clasped both paws behind her back and spun to look at him. "What's your name?" she asked, taking slow strides toward the numbat while glancing back at the sword and cape.

The numbat stopped his hammering, lifted the blade with his tongs, and dipped it into a pail of water. Steam rose around his head, and he narrowed his eyes to protect them. He placed the blade on the forge and looked at Fergal. "I am Waylond of Acadia, and I am not one for company."

"Oh. I'm a bit of a loner myself," Fergal said sprightly, rocking back and forth on the balls of her feet.

"Is that right?" Waylond said, a small grin forming on his muzzle.

"Yes. As a matter of fact I've been considering venturing out on my own recently." Fergal lifted her chin and walked a little closer to him.

"I see." Waylond raised his eyebrows. "So the Gabbling was your transportation, I suspect."

"Uh...uh, yes," she stammered. "I guess you could say that."

Waylond shook his head and laughed a little under his breath. "Now, how old could you be? Eight seasons perhaps?"

"Actually, I'm eight seasons and three weeks," Fergal said proudly. Searching for something more to say, she asked, "Have you lived here long?"

"Yes, as a matter of fact I have."

"And you've been alone all that time?"

"Yes."

"I see. It must get lonely."

"I have a lot to think about," Waylond said, as he walked to a small cabinet and took out a bowl filled with mushrooms and berries. He placed the bowl on a small table made from the stump of a tree and sat down. Fergal licked her lips and wiped a paw across her mouth to catch a bit of drool that was about to drip. He pointed to the seat across from him.

"Well, since you're here, maybe it's best if you have a bite to eat before you head back."

A bite to eat would be satisfying, Fergal thought, but the notion of heading back, of wandering into the dark wood after a meal, was not a pleasant one. Terrible thoughts entered her mind. The night forest was not a place she would like to be, and she had never traveled alone. She took a quick peek out the front of the shack. Perhaps if she sat long enough, and if her conversation was spirited enough, Waylond would ask her to stay, at least for the night. Should she tell him what had happened? No, she couldn't. He'd make fun of her, just like her brothers.

After much thought she simply said, "Thank you. I am a bit famished." Fergal climbed onto the chair opposite Waylond. Looking into his eyes, she said, in her most gracious tone, "A little tuck would hit the spot."

They ate in silence. Fergal's hope for lively conversation flowed away like the waters of the Gabbling. She was stunned, sitting there before the awesome numbat, at a loss for words. His eyes were intense and his paws massive. Nothing but the sounds of the forest, the hoot of an owl, or the breeze wending its way through the branches of the trees disturbed their meal.

After the last of the sun had dipped below the tree line in the distance, Waylond said, "Maybe it's best you stay the night. You can bed down over there." He pointed to a small pile of hay in the far corner of the shack. Fergal walked toward the spot and began to snuggle in. Thoughts of her mother and family flooded her mind and she tried to hold back a whimper, but it escaped. Waylond walked to her and knelt beside her. He reached out to her, touching her paw he said, "Don't worry, little one, the Guardian takes care of all the Forest's creatures."

"That's what my mother always told me," Fergal answered, wiping a tear from her eye.

Waylond nodded. "Your mother was right." He rose and walked to the wall where the sword hung, curled up on a cot beneath it, and closed his eyes.

Fergal wrapped her tail around her small body for warmth and comfort. *Well, I hadn't planned on leaving home quite this way. Mother must be frantic by now, but there is nothing I can do. I cannot change what has happened. Could this be the beginning of a new life for me, or should I try to find my way home? I might like becoming a blacksmith. Maybe Waylond can teach me the trade. You're too small,* she cautioned herself. *But I'm stubborn. I can do anything I set my mind to... maybe.* With this last uncertain thought she fell asleep.

Chapter 4

The night was clear except for an occasional cloud that wandered across the face of the moon. A small troop of black stoats marched in single file through the forest, moving warily in the darkness. Their eyes darted this way and that, checking for enemies or a stray creature that might be hiding behind a bush or tree. Enemies were everywhere, and other animals were always looking for a good meal.

Wulfgar, the leader of the group, strode at the front, stopping every so often to check on his band of miscreants. He shot a glance back at the group with his one good eye. His sightless eye was a ghostly remnant. A thick scar ran from the top of his head, through the eyelid, to the tip of his nose, the result of a close call with an ill-tempered cassowary. The loss did not bother him anymore because all his other senses had been heightened. He could hear a grasshopper flitting in the weeds, smell approaching rainstorms, and feel the vibrations from the footfalls of creatures well before they came into view.

He was a tall, lanky, strong and fearless stoat. He wore a black velvet vest with gold buttons, and his black boots rose to his thighs. A curved dagger was tucked into his belt and a sword hung at his side. He was confident, callous, and cruel beyond description. He grimaced then growled at his group of ragged creatures. He always made certain the other stoats knew who was in charge.

Wulfgar and his band roamed the forests of Sunderland with no goals other than to survive by any means possible. No creatures were safe while they scoured the forests. They had been traveling for days, growing more restless with each passing sunset. Step by step, they worked their way through the underbrush when a low grumble rose midway back in the ranks. The stoats froze and glared at the noisy culprit.

"It's just me stomach," the stoat whined, holding his paws to his belly. "It's been days since we had a morsel."

"Stop yer bellyaching!" Wulfgar warned. "Or I'll remove the stomach fer ya. Ya won't have ta worry about it then, will ya?"

All eyes turned to the hungry stoat, who bent his head, dropped his paws to his side, and stepped back in line away from Wulfgar's stare.

Wulfgar led the stoats through a rocky pass that opened up to reveal a rushing river. They walked along its bank, ignoring the reflection of the moon's rays that splashed along downstream. Wulfgar stopped, and sniffed the air, sensing the woods around him. Everyone came to a standstill. He raised one clawed paw above his head, and the troop dropped to their bellies. Flattening themselves against the ground, they snarled as they waited for Wulfgar's instructions.

"'*Tis something...I think*," Wulfgar thought. "On yer feet, ya lousy bunch!" he said in a low, stern voice. "Bunyip! Come here."

A young stoat came forward. He was small and his eyes remained glued to the ground as he moved toward Wulfgar. The rest of the group watched Bunyip, their upper lips curled. Low growls rose from their throats. Wulfgar could see fear in Bunyip's eyes. *The young stoat has much to learn*, he thought.

"Yes, sir. Yes, sir," Bunyip said, bowing before the stoat. He tried not to look into Wulfgar's eyes. The youngest of the group, he was abused and used by the others, so he did his best to keep his distance. They chose him to perform menial tasks, like fetching water and picking berries, or finding kindling for the night's fire. Since the others didn't care about him, it didn't matter if those tasks put him in harm's way. He was small and easy prey for the larger creatures that lived in the forest.

Wulfgar snapped his paw out and grabbed the young stoat by the ear.

"I sense and smell a meal nearby," he hissed. Tilting his head, he gazed up the slope that rose alongside the river. "Go up into the woods. Be my eyes; see what it is I sense." He pushed Bunyip to the ground. "We'll wait here. Hurry up!"

"Yes, sir," Bunyip said, scrambling to his feet.

Bunyip started up the slight incline. He took one quick look back. Wulfgar stood with his paw on his dagger, while the rest of the group dispersed like black wraiths slithering among the rocks and low shrubs. He would be at risk if there were dangers at the top of the slope. *Somehow, I'll get out of here. I'll leave these miserable creatures behind and forget them.*

His placed his steps with care, avoiding dry branches on the forest floor. If Wulfgar was correct, and he was most of the time, something was at the top of the hill. The smell of smoke from a small fire drifted through the leafy undergrowth. Mingling with the smoke, the scent of unfamiliar creatures reached his twitching nose. He parted the leaves before him. A small shack was leaning against a rocky hillside. Although he could not see any movement, he knew someone was there. He headed back down the slope.

Wulfgar grabbed him by the shoulders as he arrived at the bottom of the hill.

"Well, what's up there?" He frowned, shaking the small stoat.

"It's an old shack with a fire burning inside," Bunyip said.

"I don't care about the fire!" Wulfgar said. "I smell creatures. How many are there?"

"There are some creatures for sure, but I could not tell how many." Bunyip scratched his ears, then rubbed his paws together, wringing them over and over.

"You didn't see how many?" Wulfgar said. His upper lip curled, and Bunyip could see his sharp canines.

"No, sir," he replied, taking a step back from Wulfgar. "They's tucked in there real good. They's too far in for me to see."

"You can't even do a simple task right, Bunyip." Wulfgar's paw connected with Bunyip's jaw before Bunyip had a chance to duck. His head snapped to one side, and he let out a cry of pain. With his paw rubbing his muzzle, Bunyip lowered himself to the ground. Wulfgar's paw came up a second time but stopped in mid swing.

"Ah, you're not worth the effort," Wulfgar said, spitting at the ground in disgust. He looked down at the trembling stoat. Bunyip thought he saw pity in Wulfgar's one good eye. Then Wulfgar blinked

Bunyip had been traveling with the group since before he could remember. Wulfgar had told him they had found him alongside a forest trail. He was just a babe, a tiny kit, abandoned and alone. Wulfgar said he had no family. "We is all ya got and ya should be happy we took ya in." That's all Wulfgar ever said about it.

That was more than eight years ago. Since then he had learned how to survive, how to keep his head down and avoid any attention. Now, cowering at Wulfgar's feet, Bunyip thought about the family he never had and this lousy lot he had become a part of. His most fervent wish was to change this dark reality, but how?

"Follow me, you miserable animals!" Wulfgar's voice was stern, and no one would dare oppose his order. "And keep quiet!"

Wulfgar started up the slope, stopping for a moment as he passed Bunyip. "You stay beside me where I can sees ya! Do ya understand?"

"Yes, sir," Bunyip choked out, still rubbing his muzzle.

The two moved together up the slope, and the troop of stoats followed close behind. As they reached the top of the hill, Wulfgar raised his paw, halting the group. The shack came into view through gaps in the foliage. With his one keen eye, he stared out from the underbrush at the small building. Then with determined movements, he pointed to his left and to his right. With a nod to his troops, they moved out over the forest floor. Like black ooze, the stoats flowed in two directions to flank the shack.

Wulfgar and Bunyip

Chapter 5

The fire was dying. Only a few hot embers remained in the forge. An occasional pop caused a spark to fly to the earthen floor and flicker out.

Waylond woke with a start. He scanned the shack that had become his home over the years. Out here he found comfort with the local creatures, while making tools for the farmers. It had also given him time to think, to consider his responsibilities to the Forest and to try and accept all that had happened. He knew that he had delayed taking on the tasks of Guardian, but he was unsure of himself, and he was comfortable here.

A familiar smell reached his nose as he sniffed the air. Rising to his feet, he strode across the dirt floor and peered out of the shack. "*Wulfgar!*" He walked to where Fergal lay sleeping. He covered her muzzle with his paw, and when Fergal's wide eyes looked into his, he signaled for her to be still.

"We have unwelcome visitors," he whispered in her ear.

"Who?" she asked.

"I sense a number of stoats at the edge of the forest. Their leader is an old foe of mine. He's a scavenger and a bandit." He peered out of the shack. "Get up. We need to go."

Waylond walked to the wall of the shack where the cape and sword hung. He took the sword and strapped it to his back. Then, in one swift movement he lifted his cape from its peg, wrapped it around his shoulders, securing it with a gold clasp at his neck. Beneath the spot where the cape had hung was Waylond's wooden staff. He grabbed the staff with a free paw, signaled Fergal to stay behind him, and they headed out of the shack.

Before they could reach the safety of the forest, three snarling stoats bolted out of the darkness heading straight for Waylond. He swung his staff, connecting with all three at once. The stoats flew back and struck the base of a nearby tree. Two more stoats with daggers at the ready slithered into view. Eyes wide with fear, Fergal dashed across the dirt floor of the shack toward the forge. In an instant, she grabbed a paw full of hot coals, and flung them at the two stoats. They streaked toward the river with their fur smoldering.

Sparks from the hot coals ignited hay on the ground. An errant ember landed at the base of a wooden post, which held up the roof of the shack. Flames began to climb the post, devouring it and the thatched roof like hundreds of famished demons.

"This way," Waylond shouted at Fergal. They were stopped in their tracks as Wulfgar appeared before them. Wulfgar's sword was pointed at Waylond, and his stoats gathered behind him, ready to strike. Their pitch black eyes reflected the light from the moon, and their curled lips revealed knife-like canines.

"Put down the sword, stoat!" Waylond warned. "And call off your miserable cronies!"

"Waylond of Acadia! Well, well, well. It's been a long time." Wulfgar's one good eye was wide with recognition, and he opened his arms as though he might embrace Waylond. "How long has it been? I believe Roland was alive the last time I saw you." His snout stretched into a wide grin. "How's your brother, Waylond? I would have thought you had crawled into a hole and died after what happened between you and Morlund." With a cruel laugh, he shrugged and glared with a menacing look. Then his eyes were drawn to movement at Waylond's feet. "How interesting," he exclaimed, noticing Fergal. "The loner has found some company."

Waylond remained silent, staring coldly at Wulfgar. Fergal shifted at Waylond's feet rubbing her paw, which was scorched from the embers she had picked up.

"Not much to say about that, huh?" The evil stoat began pacing back and forth in front of Waylond. He stopped and placed the point of his sword into the dirt, leaned on it, and began picking his teeth with a sharp claw. "Ah, families," he sighed, examining his claws. "There's always some sort of problem, discord, disagreement." Waylond held Wulfgar's stare. "Well, you never were one for conversation." Wulfgar spit at the ground near Waylond's feet. "As sanctimonious as ever, aren't you? The Forests' creatures await the Guardian," he said in a mocking tone. A look of contempt flashed in his eyes. "I guess they'll just have to continue waiting, won't they?" He spat at the dirt once more, and waved a paw toward his troops. "Don't be a hero, Waylond. We outnumber you. We'll take what food and valuables ya got and be on our way."

"Still roaming Sunderland aimlessly, Wulfgar?" Waylond said in disgust. "Always taking what's not yours."

The Forest was as still as death, not even a sigh rustled the trees. The only sound came from the crackling inferno, which burned behind Waylond and Fergal. Moments passed as the creatures eyed one another with suspicion.

There are too many. Waylond considered what he might do. Closing his eyes, he sent a silent message to the Forest. In response, a wind blew in from the treetops and struck the ground with such force that dry loose debris, branches and dirt exploded in the stoats' faces. The group brought their arms and paws up to cover their eyes. Then the surrounding trees burst into flames, creating intense heat. The terrified stoats began to screech and yell, running in different directions, tripping over each other to escape the flames.

In one swift movement, Waylond pulled his hood over his head and picked Fergal up, tucking her safely under his arm. He took one last look at Wulfgar, who had fallen to the ground. The stoat struggled to his feet. His eyes scanned the area in front of the shack. There was nothing to be seen.

Waylond raised his eyes to the burning treetops. "Thank you for your sacrifice," he said, before he headed toward the woods. The trees at the edge of the Forest bent and separated, creating

41

an opening into which he and Fergal disappeared. With Fergal held tightly against him, he ran deep into the night while the screams of the stoats faded behind him.

Waylond put many miles between them and the old shack. He came to a stop on a hill overlooking a meadow. In spite of their encounter with the stoats, it was a beautiful night and Waylond gave silent thanks to the Forest for helping them escape. The moon hung low on the horizon, and its radiance covered the ground with a ghostly light. Stars burned like sparkling cinders against a sky as black as pitch.

"We're out of danger now," Waylond said, setting Fergal down at his feet. Standing beside Waylond, still within the safety of his cape, Fergal's little body shook as though her bones might fall into a heap right then and there. "Let's find some shelter so I can look at that paw of yours."

Fergal nodded. She lifted a shaking paw to rub her eyes and looked out across the meadow and up to the moon. "I'm cold," she said in a whisper.

"Yes, there's a chill." The air hummed, and the wind caressed the fur around Waylond's eyes. The leaves at the tops of the trees twisted and swirled in unison. His ears straightened up at the sounds the Forest sent him. He listened carefully to the voices of Verdigris. "We'll rest until dawn in that thicket." Placing his paws on Fergal's shoulders, he turned her, helping her to move forward. As they passed through the brush, it touched Waylond. It lingered for a second on his head, paws, and coat. It gave way to them, closing silently after they passed through. In the center of the thicket, there was enough room for them both to relax and recover. Soon they settled within the safety of its leafy walls. Waylond removed his cape and set his sword and staff on the ground beside him.

"Let me see that paw." Waylond reached out to Fergal. "What made you grab those embers?" He examined the injured paw as he spoke. From his vest he pulled out a small container. Opening it, he took a bit of the yellow cream and said, "Hold still, Fergal. This will help."

"Ouch!" She pulled her paw back. "I didn't know what else to do," she said, wincing. "I was afraid they would hurt us, or worse." She looked at Waylond. "What did that stoat mean when he said that the Forest waits for the Guardian? My mama always spoke of the Guardian of the Forest. He's supposed to watch over all of us. Why would we have to wait for him? Wasn't he watching over us tonight?"

Waylond smiled, ignoring Fergal's question. "There's more to you than meets the eye, my young friend."

"I'm okay, really I am." Fergal's eyes lacked the conviction of her words. She scratched her head with her good paw. "What happened, Waylond? The trees burst into flames around us. I've never seen anything like that."

Waylond hesitated a moment, thinking about their encounter with the stoats. "There are many things about the Forest that we don't understand." Relaxing, he leaned back on his haunches, covered the container of cream, and tucked it back into his vest. "We'll be safe tonight. We'll head out in the morning."

"Head out? Where to? Where are we?" The questions came in quick succession from the puzzled little quoll. She stared down at her wounded paw, and then she thrust her good paw deep into her pocket.

"What do you have in your pocket, Fergal?" Waylond asked.

Fergal slowly pulled her paw out, and opening it, she revealed the acorn. "It was a gift from my mother."

Waylond took it from Fergal and examined it. "It's beautiful."

"Mother always said, even though I'm tiny like this acorn, I'm still special and can do great things."

Waylond bent forward and stared into Fergal's eyes. "Your mother is right. You are special." Waylond placed the acorn back in Fergal's paw, and he closed her claws tightly around it. "Sleep now. We will talk more when the sun rises." Speaking without words to the surrounding Forest, Waylond laid a paw on Fergal's head. A warm breeze whistled down from the treetops. Fergal's eyes blinked once, then once more. Curling up beneath Waylond's watchful gaze, she closed her eyes and fell asleep.

Chapter 6

Fergal woke, rubbed the sleep from her eyes, stretched and gazed up at the grey sky. Wisps of fog moved through the air forming circles above her. She glanced down at her injured paw. It was better than new.

"Good morning, Waylond," Fergal said through a yawn. "Look, my paw is fine."

"Good morning, Fergal. Yes, it looks good."

Fergal smiled up at him. "You've been up a while, haven't you?"

He was alert and yet seemed deep in thought.

"Did you sleep well?" Fergal asked.

"Yes, very."

"I dreamt of another numbat. One just like you, but older." She paused then continued. "He had a kind face, and he told me not to worry." Waylond smiled at Fergal, and she shuffled a bit closer to him, and said, "Did that really happen? I mean, last night?" Her eyes widened. "It seems like it was just a bad dream. I was so frightened."

"No, it was not a dream, Fergal," he said. "But it's okay now."

"Oh, I see." Waylond's comforting words did not calm her. She was struck by the reality of it all. The previous night's terror came crashing down upon her, and she could feel it rise from her gut and catch in her throat. She was frightened, and her words tumbled out. "Where am I? What have I done? How can I get home? I'm just a small quoll." She jumped up, faced Waylond, and moved her paws from her neck down toward her feet. "Look at me! I'm dull," she said. "I'm not even a good quoll! I can't climb like a quoll or jump like a quoll. I don't even look right. Look at my fur. Look at my spots. My nose is not pink enough. My brothers were right. I'm dull. I'm weak and I can't do anything right 'cause *I'm* not right."

"Fergal, Fergal. Calm down." Waylond's paws waved up and down trying to shush Fergal. "We need to talk, and talk calmly. Sit." Waylond rested his paws on her shoulders and gently pushed, settling her on the ground. "Please, Fergal. Sit down."

"Ok," Fergal said, sniffling, and swiping at the tears that fell from her eyes.

"We're far from the Gabbling, and it's not safe to go back that way." Waylond held Fergal's stare, and continued. "I'm afraid that you will have to stay with me for a while, at least until the danger passes. As to where we are, I'm not entirely sure myself."

"Okay," Fergal muttered, casting her eyes to the ground.

"And what's all this talk about dull spots, not so pink noses, and weakness?" Waylond asked. "It was no weak moment that caused you to pick up burning embers. It was strength and courage."

Fergal gazed up at Waylond, searching his face for any hint of mockery. When there was none to be found, she said, "Oh, Waylond, I want to be strong, but I don't know if I can be. I want to be fearless, but I'm so afraid."

"We…all have fears, Fergal." He paused as if searching for the right words. "Inner demons. And other kinds of fear." He looked past her as if seeing something far away or, maybe something long ago. "I have mine as well…" Fergal thought she could see a deep sadness in his eyes.

"Waylond?"

"Yes, Fergal?"

"Why did we have to run away?"

Waylond looked down, avoiding Fergal's eyes. "Run away?"

"Yes, from the stoats. Why did we run? I know you could have taken them on." Fergal took a step closer to Waylond and studied him. Then she noticed the sword lying on the ground beside him. "Why didn't you use the sword or even that old wooden staff? The sword is only missing a piece in the hilt. You could have used it against the stoats." Fergal stood and struck a fencing pose. A make-believe sword was in her paws and she shuffled nimbly before Waylond, parrying with an imaginary foe. "You could have killed them all!" She ended with a final swing, spinning with a flourish.

"The sword...it's not time!" Waylond hissed, with frustration evident in his voice.

Stunned by his harsh tone, Fergal stopped, frozen on her feet, staring at him.

"But, then what's the sword for?" she asked.

"It's difficult to explain." Waylond blinked, his behavior softened, and he appeared to shrink into himself. "I don't expect you to understand."

Fergal sensed Waylond's hesitation. Was it fear or sadness?

"Waylond? What do you have to be afraid of? You're the biggest and strongest numbat I've ever seen."

As Waylond turned to look at Fergal, a voice was heard outside the thick shrub. Unaware of their presence within the thicket, a small creature was scurrying aimlessly around the bushes, talking out loud to himself.

"Oh my! Oh my! What to do! What to do!"

It circled the thicket several times and as it passed close to where they sat, Waylond thrust a paw through the bushes, grabbed the little creature and drew him in, holding him up off the ground.

"Oh my! Oh my!" it squealed. "Please don't hurt me!"

The frightened animal trembled in Waylond's firm grip. Its eyes were shut tight, and its thin legs and long tail hung down, long and limp.

"Please don't hurt me!" the creature pleaded.

"It's a bilby, Waylond," Fergal said. She reached out and tugged on the bilby's long tail. "Hey, who are you?" she asked.

"And what are you doing? You must have circled the thicket three or four times."

The animal opened his eyes and wiggled his pointy pink nose.

"If ya mean me no harm, sir," he said to Waylond, "please put me down."

A grin formed on Fergal's face. "Seems like you have a habit of picking up stray critters, Waylond."

"Humph." Waylond lowered the small mouse-like marsupial to the ground.

Standing there before Waylond and Fergal, the tiny creature said, "I am Simkin." He smoothed out his green coat and brushed bits of dirt from his pants. His head was circled with a bright blue band of fabric, and a small silver charm hung from it. Long stiff ears rose from beneath the blue band. "I have no time." After fussing with his attire, he looked directly into Fergal's eyes. "I can't stay to chat," he said. "I have to go." Simkin headed out of the thicket.

"Whoa! What's the big hurry?" Waylond asked. He grabbed the back of Simkin's collar, but Simkin twisted out of his grip and faced him.

"I was supposed to… I was sent out to…" Simkin's voice cracked. He grimaced and wrung his paws. His eyes filled with tears and he began to sob. A paw went to his mouth, and he began biting his claws. Waylond looked at Fergal uncomfortably as if pleading for her to help. Letting out a little sigh, Fergal wrapped an arm around Simkin's shoulder.

"Don't bite your claws," Fergal said. "It's a terrible habit that's hard to break."

Simkin relaxed a bit at Fergal's touch and her soothing tone.

"Take it easy. Take your time," Fergal said. "Tell us what's wrong. Maybe we can help."

Simkin fell to the ground, buried his face in his paws, and began to cry again.

"No one can help now," he wailed. "They're gone. They were counting on me, and I failed them."

Fergal sat down beside troubled bilby. He trembled all over. "What can we do, Waylond?" Fergal asked.

"I'll go get some water for him," Waylond said. "You stay here. See what you can learn. I'll be right back." He slipped out between the shrubs, leaving Fergal with Simkin.

"Can you tell me what happened?" Fergal asked with concern.

His chest heaving, Simkin slowly raised his head. He ran his paws from his eyes to the tip of his nose. Then he rubbed the remaining tears away.

"I'm from a village called Thistlewaite." His smile quivered as he spoke. "My family," he stuttered, "my extended family, and my friends live there together. We are...were...peaceful, hardworking creatures," He said. "Then they came. They came in the night when we were resting." He looked up to the brightening sky overhead. Turning to Fergal, his eyes widened with fear. "We are small creatures and we were no match for them." He shook his head, his paws clenched into fists. "We saw them. My mother told me and Bede, my brother, to run.

'Get help' she said. 'Find help.'" He shook his head again. "I should never have left her. My brother stayed behind to protect Mother. Maybe I could have done something if I had stayed." He said, as Fergal rubbed his back.

"It's alright," she said. "I'm here. No worries, my friend."

Waylond returned with a reed he had filled with water. "Take a sip, Simkin. It will help to calm you." With an appreciative nod Simkin took a swallow.

"I'm sorry. You must forgive me. I have been wandering for several days now." Simkin looked down at the ground. "I don't even know where I am. I don't know how far from Thistlewaite I am, and I don't know what to do."

"We will help you, but you have to tell us everything," Waylond said.

"Ours was not the first village to be attacked," Simkin said, a tear welling up in his eye. "There have been others; Lilydale, Fitzroy, and Jollimont. I'm not sure where they take everyone, but I do know they are shackled, and dragged away. The villagers were defenseless," he said, his paws folding across his chest over his heart. "The darkness was thick. There was no moon, and they were as black as sin." He moved his paw through the air and stared vacantly into the distance, seeming to follow some unseen shadows. "They moved like black smoke on the wind. They went through the village so swiftly. I could barely see them. They stole into our homes, dragging out the helpless bilbies and dibblers!" His voice rose with fear and terror, and he began to shake all over like the leaves on a boab tree in a windstorm.

"Who came, Simkin?" Fergal asked. A sighing wind blew in and the surrounding bushes trembled as it passed through. "Do you have any idea where they are taking them?"

"The dark ones," Simkin hissed under his breath. "They are the devil."

Waylond holds Simkin

Chapter 7

Bunyip whimpered beneath a pile of dry leaves. They crackled every time he moved, and the twigs beneath him snapped when he rolled over. He hadn't slept last night. His fear that the other stoats would catch up to him gripped him like a claw and would not allow sleep to come. They would kill him. Wulfgar would kill him. He was certain of it. *Perhaps they have found my footsteps in the woods and are following my path.* His eyes were wide with fear, and the thought of them sent a shiver up his spine. He closed his eyes. Not seeing meant not knowing, he thought. *I mustn't let myself think about it.*

Now, with dawn breaking, the events of the night before played over in his mind. Curled up into a ball under the debris at the base of a giant gum tree, he thought of the numbat who had recognized Wulfgar. He looked fearsome and unafraid, but unlike Wulfgar he seemed reluctant to fight. Bunyip recalled the small quoll at the numbat's feet. The quoll's eyes were round with fright, but the numbat protected her. *I needed to be protected.*

He wrapped his paws across his chest and hugged himself. *No one is here to protect me now.*

Last night, with sparks flying and the scent of acrid smoke stinging their nostrils, the stoat pack had confronted the huge numbat. Wulfgar taunted the marsupial as if he knew him. Or knew something important about him and his family. Bunyip's lip curled at the thought of the stoat, and a deep growl rolled up from his throat. He wondered what it was Wulfgar knew.

Whatever it was, the numbat did not give Wulfgar the satisfaction of responding to his insults.

The shack started to burn, and the forest went up in flames. It was all so quick and unexpected. The stoats tripped and fell over each other as they ran in every direction, trying to escape the heat and fire. The screams filled the night, and their faces were frozen in astonishment as they dashed away in dread. Wulfgar was tossed to the ground by the powerful wind.

Bunyip had rolled into the underbrush away from the dreadful fires, and then stumbled into the forest. He ran until he could run no more.

His running ended here, beneath this old gum tree. He was alone for the first time in his life, and he would rather die on this spot than seek help from the pack. He would rather starve than suffer more abuse from them. He would never bow and scrape to Wulfgar again. Firm in his decision, he erupted from beneath the leaves and kicked the twigs and dirt beneath his feet

I'll move westward, he thought. He hoped to meet other stoats, kinder stoats, stoats that lived out their lives in harmony with the forest and its inhabitants. "Isn't that the way it ought to be?" he asked aloud. Then he shuddered and sat back down, hiding behind a rock at the base of the tree.

The skies were grey, and the dampness of the morning air seeped through his fur to his skin, making him shudder from the top of his head to tip of his tail. Before him was an open meadow. Blades of tall grass broke the monotony of the green surface. *I'll have to cross that big field.* It was the only way to put distance between him and the pack. He would be out in the open until he reached the cover of the trees on the other side, but he needed to do this. *I can do it.* He hesitated, glancing back in the direction he had come from the night before. He looked back at the meadow, more determined than ever. The grass swayed in a slow moving breeze, and he eyed it cautiously, searching for black fur that might be hidden within it.

A kookaburra's laugh broke the silence.

"Thinking of crossing the meadow?" the bird cackled.

Bunyip looked up, spotting the bird sitting on a branch of the gum tree. "What's it to ya?" he replied through clenched teeth.

"Now, now. No need to take your troubles out on me, young man!" The bird dropped to a branch closer to Bunyip. "I'm just giving you a warning. Crossing the meadow can be dangerous." He lifted his black-feathered head, his beak directed to the grey sky, and laughed again.

Bunyip watched the kookaburra's throat vibrate out its chatter. *How wonderful it would be to have wings. I'd spread my wings and fly across the meadow. Nothing could harm me.* He narrowed his eyes as dark thoughts of his time with the stoat pack engulfed him, taking hold of his heart and squeezing out the little bit of good that remained. A bubble of unspent rage rose to his throat and he shook his fist at the bird. He screamed at it as if it were Wulfgar himself.

"What do you care what happens to me? You can't protect me. I'm nothing to you." Then, his anger spent, Bunyip's shoulders slumped and he cast his eyes to the ground. "No one cares what happens to me," he said softly.

"Why not?" The bird blinked and shook his head slowly, dropping down a branch closer to Bunyip.

"Cause they just don't." Every muscle in his body tightened. He pushed his dreams of family and love into the darkest part of himself. Those thoughts only made him weak. "I don't have to explain myself to you." Bunyip jabbed a claw in the bird's direction. "Or anyone else for that matter."

"You're right." The bird stared intently down at Bunyip. "What's your name, young stoat? Mine's Wilbing."

Bunyip didn't answer for a moment. He looked out across the open meadow, focusing on the undergrowth at the edge of the wood on the far side. *If I run fast enough, I can reach it.*

"Bunyip," he said under his breath. "My name's Bunyip." He raised his head to look at the regal bird sitting on the branch above him.

"You're on the run, young stoat." The kookaburra's black eyes blinked at Bunyip. "That much I can see."

"Humph."

"There's no one behind you. Not for miles," said Wilbing. The bird hopped down to another branch even closer to

Bunyip. Nearly eye-to-eye with Bunyip, he said, "You must cross the meadow. Be quick about it. Don't stop. Keep moving. There's much to fear in this land—things even more frightening than a band of spineless stoats."

"What would you know about it?"

"Stories travel fast in the air over Sunderland." The bird pointed to the grey sky. Then he lowered his wing and gazed at Bunyip before continuing. "You seem to have had a terrible night." He touched Bunyip's head with his wing tip. "There may be bigger challenges ahead."

"Right now, all I can think about is getting safely across the meadow," Bunyip said with a sharp tone.

"I will help you," Wilbing said, "if only to show you that some creatures do care." He puffed out his feathers. "Bunyip, you clearly have courage, but you must learn to trust." Pulling himself up and stretching his neck out, he spread his wings and sprung from the branch.

Bunyip talks to Wilbing

Chapter 8

Bunyip watched the kookaburra beat its wings and disappear over a hill. He growled to himself. *The bird was just tricking me. He won't be coming back to help.* Then he heard the bird's call and the flapping of wings overhead.

"This way!" the bird cried. "Now!"

Bunyip shot from the safety of the forest, as if he had been jabbed by a hot poker. He entered the meadow, running and leaping as fast as he could. The sunlight broke through the clouds, and its rays pierced his eyes. Running blind, he slid on moist earth and tripped over rocks. All he knew was he was moving in the general direction of the forest on the far side.

Wilbing continued to encourage him from above. "Keep running! Don't stop!" The cackling call helped to direct him. Bunyip soared over a small log that appeared in his path. The trees came closer and closer.

The loud shriek of a bird pierced the air, and Bunyip chanced a quick look up, thinking he would see Wilbing.

Instead, the giant wings of a wedge-tailed eagle blocked the sun. Panic set in. Bunyip tripped, fell and began to roll. The ground sloped downward and momentum carried him. His feet kicked out, but they could not stop him. The sky and earth flashed by as he continued to roll. He reached out, trying to grasp anything that might slow his movement. Out of control, Bunyip continued to plunge down hill. Still rolling, he struck a large rock, and then a dead branch, which slowed him. A final thump against the stump of a dead tree sent him soaring. He shut his eyes, and prepared for the sudden stop that was sure to come. Green arms caught him and held him fast. When he opened his eyes he saw a broad green leaf floating above him. A pink-colored fruit hung beneath the leaf. He was caught in the center of some sort of huge shrub. He stared once more at the pink fruit, and that's when the pain began. Something was stinging him. Every part of him was on fire.

Bunyip let out a horrific scream, and the terrified birds in the surrounding trees shrieked as they took flight. He struggled to free himself from the clutches of the shrub, but his movements caused the bush to hold him tighter and sting him again and again. Exhausted from his struggles, he stopped grappling with the bush. He could feel his eyes and snout swelling. It was becoming hard to breath, and he moaned with the effort. Once more he fought, flailing his arms and legs. He closed his eyes. *There's no one to help me*, he thought. *No family, no friends.*

Waylond and his two small companions stood at the top of a low hill overlooking the meadow. His father would have had a plan, but Waylond didn't have time for plans when he had these two small ones to care for, as well as finding Simkin's missing family. There were greater duties pressing on him. A rustling in the treetops lining the meadow caught his attention. The morning breeze whispered through the leaves. Their silvery undersides flashed in the growing light. His ears twitched in a silent reply. *I know I can't leave them*, he agreed with the wind. *If even the least of Sunderland's creatures is in danger, I must help.* With a heavy sigh, he lifted his paw to the treetops. *Thank you. I hear you.*

"Look," Fergal exclaimed. "Someone's running across the meadow."

Waylond watched the movement through the tall grass. "Yes, I see. Someone is heading toward the tree line." Looking to the sky, Waylond added, "Whoever it is had better move quickly. That wedge-tailed eagle is on the hunt."

One moment the movement was there, and then it ended with a blood-curdling screech. A flock of birds jetted to the sky. Then there was silence.

"Something terrible has happened," Simkin squeaked, and a paw went to his mouth. Fergal reached up and removed the paw before Simkin could start to bite.

"Come on," Waylond said. "We'll find out what's going on." With Waylond in the lead, the three companions headed down to the forest on the far side of the meadow.

"It was right around here somewhere," Fergal said as she scanned the thick undergrowth. "But I don't see anything."

Waylond stood alert, his brow furrowed as he carefully scanned the woods. "There!" He pointed toward a large leafy shrub. "Stay here."

Waylond walked toward the dark green bush and stopped short a few feet away.

"A stinging bush," he said. He began to circle the bush slowly, keeping a safe distance from the broad, heart-shaped leaves. On the far side of the bush two legs stuck out from beneath a limb. The upper body of the creature was hidden under the plant.

Fergal gasped. "What is it?"

"It's a dead body," Simkin said flatly.

"Maybe it's not dead," Fergal said.

"Yes it is!" Simkin countered, twisting his paws into a knot. "We shouldn't touch it. That's a dangerous thing to do."

"Stop it, the both of you, and step back!" Waylond warned. "I told you to stay over there!" The sound of moaning drifted out from beneath the shrub.

"Oh, it is alive," Fergal said. Taking a step forward, she came to an abrupt stop, held fast to the spot by Waylond's powerful arm.

"Stay here, Fergal. I told the two of you to step back, and I meant what I said. This is no ordinary forest shrub. This is a gympie-gympie."

"A gympie-gympie?" Fergal and Simkin asked at the same time.

"Yes, and it's poisonous." Waylond lowered himself to the ground for a better look. Another moan came from the creature. Waylond bent beneath the leaves of the shrub and reached for the creature's feet. Clasping the ankles, he pulled, trying to free the animal from the clutches of the gympie-gympie. With a loud snap, the shrub's branches released their hold.

"It's a stoat," Simkin said. "His snout and eyes are swollen."

"Yes, the poison from the bush causes swelling." Waylond examined the injured stoat, who peered at them through puffed up eyes. Waylond lifted him off the ground and carried him away from the shrub. He laid the stoat down on a moss-covered mound beneath a tingle tree and reached into his jacket to pull out the small container that held the sticky yellow cream.

"Isn't that what you put on my paw?" Fergal asked.

"The same." Waylond smiled. "The gympie-gympie delivers a burning sting. This will help." Waylond applied the cream to the stoat's snout and around his eyes. Finally, he placed a drop onto the injured stoat's tongue. Soon the swelling began to diminish, and the young stoat was able to open his eyes better. Startled by the three creatures sitting before him, the stoat bolted up and back-pedaled on his butt until the trunk of the tingle tree stopped his movement.

"Oooh ah ya gus?" His swollen tongue did its best to form the words. His lips were so swollen that what he said came out a bit garbled, but he was making himself perfectly clear. "Wa a minnt. I know yas." He pointed to Waylond, then to Fergal. "Las nigh, the sha…"

"Oh, you're the young stoat that was with that nasty bunch last night. Yes, we were there," Fergal said. "And it's a good thing we were here too. We just rescued you from that nasty shrub."

"Yes, yes," Simkin stuttered. "It stung you. Waylond pulled you out." Simkin pointed a claw to Waylond, and then brought it back towards his teeth.

"Don't even think about it!" Fergal said to Simkin. Her steely look was enough to make him lower his paw.

"What's your name?" Fergal asked the stoat.

"The name's Bunyip," he said with a sour tone, his words coming a bit clearer. Struggling to his feet, he leaned back against the tree and rubbed his paws over his eyes, snout and head. "I don't know what you guys want, but I don't need your help."

"Well then, we'll just put you back where we found you," Fergal said, with a grin. "If it wasn't for Waylond you'd still be under that gympie whatever." She tilted her head up to Waylond. "He's ungrateful. Let's just leave him here."

"That's not like you, Fergal," Waylond said.

"Well," she said, eyeing the stoat with suspicion, "I know, but he's so...so, rude."

"Hmm, maybe you're right." Waylond said. "What do you think, Simkin?"

"He makes me nervous." Simkin shrugged. He began to raise a claw to his mouth and then, glancing at Fergal, flashed a small grin and tucked his paw into his pocket. "He's trouble."

Waylond looked at Fergal, then to Bunyip, and back again. He shook his head and said, "You're welcome to come with us, Bunyip. You look like you might be on the run. I don't know where you were going, and I'm not certain where we are heading, but you'll be safe with us. You seem a bit young to be wandering in the forest alone. Where's your family?"

"I have none," Bunyip said with anger in his voice. "I can take care of myself." He folded his arms across his chest and looked away.

"We'll honor your decision but feel free to follow," Waylond offered. *He must make his own decisions and live with them,* Waylond thought. *He must find his own path. And so must I.* He looked back at Bunyip. *I think I know what his decision will be,* he thought, before leading Fergal and Simkin farther into the wood.

Chapter 9

Fergal and Simkin followed in Waylond's footsteps. They had been hiking uphill all day and the two were tired. Fergal watched as Waylond put down each paw and strode ahead, his staff striking the ground after each step.

Simkin was at Fergal's side, tugging on her jacket. "My feet hurt," he complained.

"Mine too," Fergal said. "I'm wondering what Waylond is thinking."

"He's working out a plan to help find my family," Simkin nodded. He was now certain that Waylond would help.

"That would be good, Simkin," Fergal said. She stopped in her tracks and Simkin stopped too. She studied her new friend. Although they hadn't known each other long, she felt protective of him, like she was the big sister and he was her little brother. "It would be good to find your family." She rested a paw on his shoulder. "But it would also be nice if Waylond could help me get back home to mine." In his eyes she saw concern and sadness. "First we'll find yours, of course." A slight smile shone on his face. She looked up the path. "He's getting ahead of us. Let's hurry."

"Look, Waylond," Fergal said when she and Simkin caught up to him. "The forest is thinning out."

"Yes. It's the high country," he replied.

"Have you figured out how are we going to rescue my family?" Simkin asked.

"I'm not sure, Simkin," Waylond replied. "We don't know exactly where they've been taken."

"Don't worry, Simkin. Waylond will help," Fergal said. "Just look at what he did for that nasty stoat."

"Fergal, we know nothing about that stoat," Waylond said. "Sometimes it's difficult to understand a creature unless you've walked on their life's trail."

"You're right, but you did pull him out of the gympie-gympie, and he seemed ungrateful." Fergal looked up at Waylond. "What do you think he is doing now?"

"I think he's following us," Waylond said, as he walked forward with a steady step.

Simkin and Fergal snapped to attention. They both stared back down the path into the depths of the Forest.

Fergal narrowed her eyes and peered into the trees. "I don't see anything," she said.

"Me neither," said Simkin.

"Oh, he's there. Trust me," Waylond assured them. "He's a stealthy little stoat."

The late afternoon sun was bright, and the terrain ahead was dry and rocky. On their left a stand of scrawny trees stood a lonely vigil. To their right a cliff dropped off to a rushing river hundreds of feet below. Mt. Olga rumbled in the distance, its volcanic peak belching black smoke into the sky. Straight ahead stood a group of huge boulders. On the right side of the boulders, a narrow path along the cliff's edge led down to the valley below.

"This is Windjana Gorge." Waylond stared out across the gorge to Mt. Olga. "If I remember correctly, there is a bridge over the gorge. Perhaps we should use it to cross to the other side. There, we will be able to find shelter within the boundaries of the forest. We need to consider our next move. The land ahead is rocky and barren. Crossing the gorge to the forest on the other side seems like the best choice. We are in the open here." He looked down at Fergal. A frown flickered across his lips. "And we need to make a plan. Simkin's family needs us to find them."

"The bridge is guarded with more guards than you can fight." The voice came from behind them. Waylond, Simkin and Fergal turned to see Bunyip's skinny frame leaning against a leafless, skeletal tree.

"So glad you could join us, Bunyip," Waylond said.

"I didn't think we would see you again," said Fergal.

"So you know a bit about the bridge," Waylond said, taking a step toward the young stoat. "Am I right?"

"Yes, I do know something about the bridge," Bunyip said. He snapped a dead twig from the thin tree and began to chew on it. "Wulfgar talked about the bridge all the time." His smug look disappeared, and he dropped the twig to the ground. "The bridge is nothing compared to that mountain. I know what's happening beneath that mountain." He pointed toward Mt. Olga. "It's not just a threatening volcano. They are doing awful things in there."

"Who? What kinds of things?" Waylond furrowed his brow and gazed at Bunyip.

"They are using slaves to mine something down there." Bunyip blinked, scratched his head, and looked into Waylond's eyes.

"My family," Simkin whimpered.

Fergal moved closer to him and placed her arm around him. "That's awful. Do you think Simkin's family is somewhere beneath the mountain, Waylond?" Fergal asked.

"It sounds like a good possibility." Waylond said. "If they are there, we must to try to get in and rescue them. How do you know all this, Bunyip?"

"Wulfgar spoke of it often. I can tell you that if you're planning to go in there you're crazy. You're putting yourself and your two friends at risk," Bunyip replied gesturing toward the gorge. "Nedra's troops are at the bridge, so you can't go that way. They cover the bridge like flies."

"Nedra? Who's Nedra?" Fergal asked.

"She's the white devil," Bunyip said in a low voice. "She lives deep in the mountain. Some say that she has never seen the sun."

As if in response, the sun slid behind Mt. Olga's peak and its shadow fell over them. They had been traveling most of the day, and evening was beginning to fall. Fergal shivered as she pulled her jacket tighter around her. "It's getting cold, Waylond," she said. "If Bunyip is right, and the bridge over the gorge is guarded, what will we do? Is there another way to get to that mountain?"

Waylond peered out toward the smoking peak.

"Bunyip, do you know for sure that there are slaves beneath the mountain?" Waylond focused on Bunyip. "Are you certain about what's happening there? Do you know a way to get in?"

"I'm sure. Wulfgar doesn't lie about stuff like that." Bunyip tipped his chin up. "I know what I'm talking about, and it doesn't matter to me if you don't believe me. I know there are gateways through the caverns in Mt. Olga. That's how they bring slaves down to the center. I know a lot of stuff you guys don't know."

"Oh my," Fergal said. "You are cheeky. Did you forget how we helped you?"

Fergal watched Waylond as he stared at the volcano in the distance. A moment passed as everyone listened to Simkin mumbling to himself in his usual worried fashion.

"Since it's getting late, we'll stay here for the night. We all need some rest."

"We'll get them out. Won't we, Waylond?" Fergal asked.

"We'll find a way," Waylond said quietly.

"Humph. I'll go with you just so I can see this," Bunyip said, with a smirk. "By the way, you do know that they are not far behind, don't you?"

"What are you talking about, Bunyip?" Fergal demanded.

"Yes, I do know," Waylond said. "But the stoats won't catch up with us tonight. And they're not really looking for us, are they, Bunyip?"

Bunyip lowered his eyes to the ground and said nothing. Waylond waited a moment for a response. When none came, he walked to a small group of trees and settled down at the base of one. Looking up into the tree, he watched the wind as it swept through the leaves. He motioned to Fergal and Simkin to sit with him.

When Fergal and Simkin were sleeping contently beside him, Waylond turned to Bunyip. "Tell me more about Mt. Olga," he said. Darkness had fallen, and a crescent moon was on the rise.

"I've pretty much told you everything I know," Bunyip said.

"Then tell me something else," Waylond said leaning closer to the young stoat. "Tell me something you suspect or may have heard the stoats talking about."

"I think...maybe I...wait, I heard some of them talk about the mining."

Waylond looked up to the night sky. "What about the mining?" he asked.

"Well," Bunyip began. "Wulfgar says that Nedra likes the precious gems dug up from deep within the mountain."

"Is there more?" Waylond said, his eyebrows rose in surprise.

Bunyip rubbed his nose, his black eyes sparkled and his forehead wrinkled with thought. "It just doesn't make a lot of sense to me. It is said that Nedra has more precious stones than she can wear, but she keeps mining for more."

"Yes," Waylond agreed. "That is a bit strange."

"Wulfgar is not afraid of anything, but once I heard him mock Nedra. He said she was a foolish nothing. He said there was another creature there, a powerful creature, more frightening than even Nedra. He had heard things about it. He doesn't know who or what it is. But whenever he mentioned it I saw fear in his eyes. It was only for a moment, but it was there."

"Another creature?" Waylond leaned toward Bunyip and spoke in a low tone. "What is this other creature?"

"Like I said, Wulfgar doesn't know who or what it is. But I can tell you, he's scared, and that's saying a whole bunch." Bunyip looked around as if he expected something or someone to jump out from behind a tree or a rock. "If Wulfgar is scared, then I think we should be running from Mt. Olga as fast as we can."

"No, Bunyip. We can't run or hide anymore," Waylond said with determination.

Chapter 10

The hoot of an owl woke him. It was the middle of the night, and the air was still, but Waylond felt an odd sensation at his back. He had fallen asleep leaning against a tree and now it began to vibrate, sending small shockwaves through his spine to his chest. It made his fur stand on end. He looked up into the tree, but saw nothing there.

He checked his three young companions, who were all sleeping soundly. He tried to relax, but thoughts kept flowing through his mind like the current of a rushing river, and he could not stop the torrent. The vibrations began to change into soft murmurings, which caught his attention. When he looked up again, there was movement. The leaves and branches twisted and swayed as though caught in the night's wind, but the surrounding trees were still. The air moved only above Waylond. As the branches danced, he caught a glimpse of the brilliant crescent moon shining between them. The murmurings grew into whispers, and he scanned the leaves above him for its source. The foliage shifted, and the faint sound of voices made his ears twitch. Faces seemed to appear, laced together with twigs and bits of greenery in the treetop. Small pieces of the tree showered around him. The Verdigris was looking down on him. The Guardians of the past were with him.

"Tell me. What should I do?" There was no answer, just whispers in the wind. "Should I go to the mountain?" The whispers grew louder, and the faces in the leaves smiled slightly. "I know I have to complete the sword, but I don't know where Morlund is, and he has the crystal."

"Go through the Styx," the Verdigris murmured.

"The Styx is a dangerous place for the young ones. I have no power there, and I don't know what we will find."

The whispering grew louder. "Go to the mountain through the Styx. There is no other way. You will meet your destiny beneath the mountain. The Forest and generations of past Guardians have spoken. You have been given the gifts and powers you will need to succeed. You have forged the sword. You must now accept your responsibility and recognize who you are. Join the sword with the crystal."

"The time is not right."

"It must be done," the voices said. "You must complete the sword and accept who you are meant to be."

The leaves separated, shifted and settled, and the faces were gone. The tree was still. He shook his head and looked at the ground. *I don't have the crystal,* he thought. *I can't complete the sword without it.*

He felt empty and frustrated with his situation. *I want to be what the Forest expects, but I have always felt inadequate and useless. I was unable to stop Morlund from taking the crystal, the very heart of the Forest and the source of power for the sword. Maybe I'm not strong enough to save Simkin's family or the other animals being held captive there. And what or who is the creature that inhibits the caverns of the mountain? If it wields unimaginable power, how will I face it?* Then it struck him. The realization sent blood rushing from his head, fear gripped his heart and squeezed it like a vise. Rage rose within him and he was filled with anger. He clutched the dagger at his waist as the answer became clear. *It's Morlund. Bunyip was speaking of Morlund. He's the other creature beneath Mt. Olga.* Closing his eyes, he calmed himself. *The past is the past; I cannot allow it to rule my decisions or me. I must not make it the driving force for what I do. I must move forward even if it means toward Mt. Olga.* "I must complete the sword," he said out loud.

Fergal's small voice broke the silence. "Why do you have to complete the sword, Waylond?"

Waylond's gaze snapped to Fergal, whose eyes glittered in the moonlight. She was wide awake and waiting for an answer.

"You should be resting, Fergal. Our long journey to the mountain begins at dawn."

"Then we're going to Mt. Olga?" Fergal asked. "You look worried. Can I help?"

"No, I don't think so, Fergal."

"You can talk to me. I'm a good listener." She placed her paw on his and smiled. "My mother always said I was a good listener." She nodded, and he could see the pride shine in her eyes.

He decided it was time to help her understand. "Fergal, you asked about the sword."

"Yes, you always carry it on your back. I wonder why you don't use it."

"It's special." He smiled. Then the smile disappeared. "It's powerful."

"Powerful?"

"Yes, it is a weapon of the Guardian of the Forest."

She stared up at him, and then, in slow motion, her mouth opened to speak. "You're him, aren't you? You're the Guardian."

"And you're a very clever girl."

"Will we go to the mountain just to find Simkin's family?"

"Yes, but I must complete the sword as well."

"The opening on the hilt," she said.

"Yes." He reached over his shoulder and drew the sword from its sheath. The blade flashed in the moonlight.

"What goes in the opening, Waylond?" she asked. She placed her paw on the blade and looked at Waylond.

"A crystal, a green crystal."

"Will it help us save Simkin's family?"

"Well, yes, but there is another reason why I must go to Mt. Olga."

"I don't understand, Waylond."

"Bunyip has warned me about a creature that Wulfgar fears?"

"What kind of creature? Do you know what it is?"

"I think…I may know who it is. I may even have had a hand in creating him."

"Waylond, how could you?" Startled, Fergal moved closer.

"The creature may be my brother. He has the crystal. The crystal gives him power, and I must get it back."

"What will you do about your brother?"

"I'll try to get him back as well."

"Because you are the Guardian and even your brother needs protection."

"That's right, Fergal, even my brother needs protection. Especially him. Now go to sleep. We have a long journey ahead."

Fergal reached up, and wrapped her arms about Waylond's neck, hugging him. "Thank you for everything, Waylond. You have been a guardian to me." She pulled away and looked into his eyes. He could see something there he hadn't seen in a long time. It warmed his soul and gave him renewed strength. He knew he would need it in the days ahead.

Chapter 11

Dawn broke over Windjana Gorge. The tops of the rugged mountains were bathed in the early sunlight. Their tips burned like orange flames scorching the morning sky. Fergal blinked, opened her eyes, and rubbed the sleep away. Simkin slept beside her and Bunyip was up wandering through the rocky landscape. He seemed to be searching for something at the edge of the forest. Then he would return to the cliff and gaze down at the rushing river below.

I wonder what he's looking for, Fergal thought. She nudged Simkin. He woke with a start, shaking his head, and blinking his eyes, he tried to adjust to the morning light.

With a yawn, he ran a paw over his head to scratch an ear.

"Everyone gather around," Waylond said.

Fergal and Simkin pulled themselves up, stretched, yawned, and walked toward Waylond and plopped at his feet. Simkin's paw rose to his mouth. Fergal grabbed it before Simkin's teeth could bite a single claw.

"Aw," Simkin complained, "I haven't bit a claw in days. Look!" he held out his paw. "Just look at how long my claws are!"

"Forget about your claws. Think about heading down into Windjana Gorge," Fergal said. "Right, Waylond?"

"That's right, Fergal."

"What do you mean head down into the gorge?" Simkin barked. "When are we going to do that?"

Bunyip focused his attention on the small group and walked to where they sat, taking a seat beside Waylond. He looked up at the numbat, and Waylond returned his gaze.

"You seem preoccupied, Bunyip. Is there something you want to share?"

"No, not really. I just…" He cast a quick look toward the forest and then at Waylond. "Nope, nothing to share."

"Well, I have something to share, and it's important," Waylond said. "To get to Mt. Olga, we cannot cross the gorge over the bridge." He looked at each one of them before continuing. "Bunyip has told us that the bridge is heavily guarded. There is another way. We will take the route through the Styx to Mt. Olga."

Bunyip laughed under his breath and shook his head.

"Is there a problem, Bunyip?" Fergal asked.

"A problem? Are you kidding me?" Bunyip scoffed. "First of all the Styx is not a place any creature wants to be. It's enchanted and evil." He looked steadily at Waylond. "Once you get to the volcano, how are you going to defeat Nedra and her troops? You'll need an army. I told you about Nedra and that other creature who has special powers. Even if you do get in there, you'll never get out alive." His eyes narrowed and the hair on his neck began to bristle. "There are powerful forces going on in there. I told you, something really strange is happening."

"We're not defenseless, Bunyip. We have real power too," Fergal said. Then she caught herself, gazed at Waylond for a moment, and shifted her eyes to the ground.

Bunyip looked at Waylond. "Power? What power?" Bunyip said. "Really? And who might that be? You?" He pointed at Waylond. "The same guy that ran away from Wulfgar the other night? Maybe this big hulking numbat here thinks he can defeat Nedra's army by himself!" Bunyip broke into laughter, but the rest of the group remained silent.

Fergal rose to her feet and began pacing. She stopped before Waylond, placed her paws on her hips, and began tapping a foot on the ground. "Tell him, Waylond. Tell him," she insisted. "You can't keep this to yourself anymore. We need you, the slaves in Mt. Olga need you, and Simkin's family needs you."

The three studied Waylond. He stood and took a step back. His tail flicked, and his eyes peered into the forest. Bunyip, Simkin and Fergal followed his stare.

"What's this all about, Waylond?" Bunyip asked.

"I am the Guardian of the Forest. I have powers of my own," he said. He continued to study the woods. Bunyip's jaw dropped.

"Fergal," Waylond said. "It's time to go. Take Simkin and hide behind those boulders." He pointed across the dry landscape to the huge stones that sat close to the cliff's edge. He looked back at the forest.

"What's wrong?" Fergal said. "You're frightening me."

"Move, Fergal. Do as I say and take Simkin with you."

Grabbing Simkin by the paw, Fergal pulled him so hard that his feet flew off the ground. He came down on one knee, managed to put his feet under him and began to run. "Let's go!" Fergal yelled. "Let's go!"

"What's happening?" Simkin said, his feet tripping as he went.

"I don't know, but it's something big." Still holding Simkin by the paw, Fergal headed toward the rocky outcropping.

The young stoat stared at Waylond with wide eyes as Waylond leaned down to pick up his staff. Waylond placed a paw on Bunyip's shoulder and their gaze shifted to the woods. In barely a whisper Bunyip said, "They're close."

"Run," Waylond ordered. Bunyip needed no more encouragement. He quickly took a step back, and began running toward Fergal and Simkin.

A stiff wind shook the trees at the edge of the forest. Waylond faced into it, his nose twitched, his fur rippled. A subtle movement just inside the tree line caught his eye. A small group of stoats poured out from the forest's depths like poison from a goblet. They were armed to the teeth, paws grasping broad swords, daggers and knives. Laughing, they threw their heads back, exposing their fangs. As the ranks parted, Wulfgar strode through. Snickering, he walked up to Waylond, stopping just a few feet from the numbat.

Fergal and Simkin peeked out from behind a boulder. Bunyip stood beside it, shaking all over. He was frozen to the spot.

"So we meet again, Waylond," Wulfgar said. "What are you and your friends doing out here in the middle of nowhere?"

"We're going to save my family!" Simkin shouted from behind the boulder. "Leave us alone."

Fergal slapped a paw over his muzzle, but it was too late.

Wulfgar looked across at the rocky outcropping where Fergal and Simkin were crouched. It was then he saw Bunyip. "Bunyip!" Wulfgar shouted. "Do ya think ya can just run away from me, boy?"

"Leave the young stoat alone, Wulfgar," Waylond said.

"Or what, great Guardian of the Forest? Or what? You are the great Guardian, aren't ya?"

Wulfgar made the first move. In a flash he slipped past Waylond and ran toward Bunyip. Wulfgar's comrades closed in on Waylond. Waylond swung his staff in a wide arc. Each time he swung, the clash of steel swords against Waylond's weapon reverberated over the cliffs and rolled like thunder to the peaks of Windjana Gorge.

Wulfgar closed in on Bunyip with claws extended. Terror seized the small stoat, and he didn't move. As Wulfgar advanced toward him, a tumble of dark brown fur shot from behind the boulder. Fergal slammed into Wulfgar with all the force she could muster. Her attack stopped his approach, but she bounced off his muscled shoulder and directly into Bunyip, who stumbled closer to the rim of the precipice, his arms windmilling as he tried to regain his balance. Fergal stretched out her paw, locking Bunyip's paw in hers, grabbing on to him as he hung off the edge. She dug in with all her might, her back paws struggling against the hard packed dirt and rock. There was nothing to hold on to and they both tumbled over the edge.

Then she heard Waylond scream, "Fergal!"

His cry clawed at her ears as she and Bunyip plummeted to the raging river below.

Chapter 12

A blood-curdling scream from Wulfgar was enough to halt the fighting. Waylond stared at the stoat, who stood motionless at the edge of the cliff. With his back toward Waylond, and his sword hanging loose at his side, Wulfgar gazed into the gorge.

"Fergal." Waylond spoke in barely a whisper, his eyes focused on the spot where she and Bunyip had disappeared.

Wulfgar turned to Waylond. "I can't see 'em," he said. "They's gone. I can't see 'em." He dropped to his knees and gazed at Waylond, his eyes glistening with tears.

Shaking, Simkin took a few timid steps out from behind the boulder toward Waylond, who placed a paw on Simkin's back as he considered Wulfgar.

Stunned by Wulfgar's behavior, Waylond said in a concerned voice, "We need to talk?"

Wulfgar's only response was a low growl.

Waylond moved to the boulder, with Simkin at his heels. Facing Wulfgar, Waylond lifted his staff and plunged it into the ground in front of him. Letting go, the staff remained buried in the earth. Then he sat down, Simkin at his side, and waited to see what Wulfgar would do.

Nearby, Wulfgar's troops stood frozen, watching him intently. With a snarl, Wulfgar waved his paw and his stoats relaxed, gathering together, they mumbled to each other.

Wulfgar stuck his chin out, shook his head and ran a paw across his muzzle.

"You're lucky," Wulfgar began. "We could be tearing you limb from limb right now." He took a step toward Waylond and sat across from him. He looked at the ground while absently running a claw through the dirt. "This should not...I can't believe..." Wulfgar began.

"Yes, I know." Waylond, said, watching Wulfgar's band of ruffians. "We have both lost someone. There's no need for bloodshed. Just leave."

"Guardian, you know nothing of loss," Wulfgar hissed.

"How did you know?" Waylond asked.

"Your brother told me you were the Guardian." Wulfgar's stare drifted to the spot where Bunyip fell. "You were too confused and unsure of ya self to take on the responsibility."

"That's not important now, Wulfgar. Do *you* want to tell me what Bunyip was to you?" Waylond asked in a low voice. "It's obvious that he wasn't just another thief."

"Watch who yer callin' thief." Wulfgar growled and removed his dagger from its sheath. Shouts of encouragement were heard from Wulfgar's stoats. "Shut up, ya motley bunch," he shouted at them. Then turning to Waylond he said, "I should slit yer throat right here and now, but I don't want ta waste me energy."

"He must have been some sort of kin," Waylond said, paying no attention to Wulfgar's threat.

"And what would ya care if he were me brother's son." Wulfgar dropped his head and shook it. He thrust the point of his dagger into the dry earth. "I told him I would care for him," he said. "I didn't want no kid. No, not me." He took in a deep breath and let out a sigh. "What could I do?" His paws spread out in appeal in front of him. "Them were his dying words. 'Take care of me son,' he said. So I been doing the best I could."

"Why didn't you tell him you were his uncle?" Waylond furrowed his brow, mystified by Wulfgar's behavior.

"Ah, ya know how it is, mate. I didn't want the kid slobbering all over me. Asking me for stuff." Wulfgar waved his paw absently in the air. "Didn't want my troops to think I'm partial 'cause he's me relation." Wulfgar looked into Waylond's eyes. "I'm an important guy. Got tons ta do ya know, ruffians ta care for." He tilted his head toward his band of miscreants. "They's ain't much, but they's been real loyal, and they's all I got." He pointed at the group of stoats, and they nodded to each other.

Wulfgar let out a growl as Simkin poked his head out from behind Waylond. "Don't be makin' any false moves, ya dolt of a bilby!" He pulled his dagger from the ground and waved it in front of Simkin's face. "Ya could get killed sneakin' up on a stoat."

"Leave Simkin alone, Wulfgar," Waylond said quietly. "He's done nothing to you."

"Yeah, he's done nothin' just like you. Nothin'. Bunyip's gone over the cliff and no one's done nothin'."

"Are you going to leave us alone now, Mr. Wulfgar?" Simkin pleaded. "There are only two of us. We can't hurt you."

"That's right, son, you can't hurt us, but we can hurt *you*."

"We have nothing," Waylond's voice was stern. "And now we are less than we were a few moments ago. Leave, Wulfgar, and you'll not have any trouble from me. Take your band of misfits with you and stop following us." Waylond cocked his head toward the group of stoats.

"Followin' ya! Ya thinks me and me men are followin' ya?" He let out a bark of a laugh. "Why would me and me boys be doing that?" Then in a whisper only Waylond could hear, he stuttered, "Do ya...do ya think he survived the fall?"

"Anything's possible," Waylond answered, shaking his head.

"Humph," was all Wulfgar replied. "So are ya gonna go to Mt. Olga?"

"Yes, we're going to try to get Simkin's family out, and the others if we can."

"Do ya really think ya can git those critters out without killing 'em or yerself?" Wulfgar asked. "I suppose the bilby there put ya up to it." Wulfgar sneered. "Cryin' little bilby tears over his bilby village."

"We're going to save my family," Simkin piped up bravely.

"You're gonna get yer whole family killed. That's what's gonna happen."

"We have to try," Waylond answered.

"Well, no skin off my nose," Wulfgar said. "The closer ya gets to Mt. Olga, the further ya gets from ever coming back. Not that I cares." With that, Wulfgar stood, turned to his men and sharply barked, "We're out!" Wulfgar and his hoard of stoats slipped back into the forest and disappeared from sight.

It hit Simkin all at once, and he dropped to Waylond's feet, sobbing. Waylond wrapped his arm around Simkin's shoulders. When he could manage it, Simkin lifted his head and looked at Waylond through his tears.

"What now, Waylond?" he sobbed. "What do we do? Who will stop me from biting my claws?" He lifted his paws and looked at his claws. "She cared about me."

"She cared about me too, Simkin."

"So what do we do now?"

"We'll do just as we were planning," Waylond said. "We'll find your family and bring them home."

Simkin had settled in, but Waylond still grappled with his plans. How would he get into the mountain, and what would he do when he was finally face to face with Morlund? He draped his cape over Simkin, who had fallen asleep in tears.

He was restless, so he rose and walked over to the edge of the cliff. He thought about Fergal and what she had meant to him, and what she had done for him. "I did not get a chance to say 'thank you,' Fergal." He bowed his head, then slowly looked at the river far below. "I promise we'll free Simkin's family. Then I'll find yours." Waylond stared at the spot in the tree line where moments ago Wulfgar and his men had disappeared. There, at the edge of the wood stood Wulfgar.

"Well, yer not gonna be able to do it alone," Wulfgar said in a gruff voice while striding toward Waylond. "We're gonna do this together. I know what yer thinking, numbat." He narrowed his eyes and pointed a sharp claw in Waylond's direction.

"Can we trust you, Wulfgar?" said Waylond. "That's what I'm thinking. You've given us no cause to do so, and I'm not sure there isn't some other motive besides mere kindness."

"Let's just say that I'm doin' it for Bunyip."

"What about your troops? What will they do?"

"They's heading home," Wulfgar said, his head tilting toward the forest. "This is not their battle. I'm responsible for Bunyip. Not them." Wulfgar hesitated a moment. "But don't think you can boss me around, numbat!"

"Okay. It's settled then."

Chapter 13

A steep path ran alongside the cliff to the base of Windjana Gorge. The sun was low in the sky before them and a chill drifted through the air. It had taken most of the day to trek down the path to the valley at the bottom. The swift river flowed by on their right. Waylond and Wulfgar gazed at it in silence as they walked beside it.

"What is the name of this cursed river?" Wulfgar asked.

"It is the Gabbling," Waylond replied. "It cuts through the realm of Sunderland."

"How could something that has taken away so much have such a delightful name?" Wulfgar said with a sneer.

Waylond stopped and looked back up the path they had traveled. Cliffs on both sides of the river soared to the sky, seeming to touch the clouds floating above them. Here, where they stood, the cliffs came to an abrupt end and a flat dry expanse of land lay before them. They would need to cross it to reach the Styx, which was a spec of green in the distance.

Smoke from the top of Mt. Olga could be seen rising over the woods. The river wound across the land and disappeared as it headed toward the Styx and the mountain.

"Do we, I mean are we…" Simkin, stammered. He looked across to the Styx in the distance. He licked his muzzle, and twisted his paws together. "Are we going into *that* place?"

Waylond glanced down at Simkin and then at Wulfgar. "Yes, we must. It's the best way to reach Mt. Olga," Waylond said. He patted Simkin on the shoulder. When he glanced up he saw Wulfgar shaking his head back and forth with his eyes fixed to the ground.

"Wulfgar, what is it?" Waylond asked. "Why are you shaking your head? Do you see a problem?"

"Nothin'," Wulfgar replied. He narrowed his eyes and twitched his nose. "I've heard the Styx strikes fear into the hearts of many." He looked back to find Waylond studying him. "But not me, of course! Not me."

"It doesn't matter what you've heard," Waylond said. "We'll find out what this place is all about for ourselves, and then we'll judge."

Waylond took a step forward. Simkin and Wulfgar fell in step behind him.

They slowed to a stop at the edge of the Styx. The immense trees seemed to lean forward, beckoning them to come closer, daring them to enter. Decaying branches overhead were caked with dripping moss. Gnarled roots twisted up through dense ferns and wrapped around the trunks of the ancient trees, attempting to choke them. This was not the Forest of the Guardians. It was a forest with forces of its own, forces Waylond was not familiar with. The air swirled around them, touching them, rippling their fur as it moved by—it was as though the Styx was a living, breathing thing, watching or tasting them. Simkin pressed up against Waylond's leg, wrapping his arms around it. Waylond's great paw dropped to Simkin's shoulder and held him.

He glanced at Wulfgar. "Are you ready?" Waylond asked.

"Ready as I'm ever gonna be," Wulfgar replied, as he pulled his dagger from its sheath and held it before him.

Pushing a giant fern aside, Waylond stepped in and held the frond back for his companions. Wulfgar passed into the forest first, followed close behind by Simkin. Once they had all entered the wood, the giant fern sprang back into place behind them like a door slamming shut in complete silence. The dry lowland they had crossed and the cliffs of Windjana Gorge were no longer in sight.

Like the trees, everything on the ground was covered in a blanket of wet moss, and with every step their feet sank in. Moisture dripped from the branches like rain. Their fur became damp, clothes clung and hung about them, and small beads of dew formed on the tips of their noses. Simkin wiped the back of his paw across his muzzle and up his face, trying his best to wipe away the water soaking through to his skin.

The Gabbling entered the Styx as well, and Wulfgar walked close to the river's edge, staring into the water. His feet sank in up to his ankles with every step. Waylond watched him scour the banks.

"The earth alongside the river is treacherous," Waylond said.

"So what do you suggest, numbat?" he asked. "If they survived the fall, maybe the river has carried them here. Maybe we should be looking for footprints."

"You're right, but it's too dangerous to be walking so close to the river."

"Then how will we find them, if they're still alive?"

"We will follow the river's path to the mountain," Waylond answered.

"Then what are we waiting for? Let's get moving." Wulfgar said, pulling a foot free of mud.

Waylond headed deeper into the woods with Wulfgar and Simkin close behind.

On they walked for what seemed like forever. They clambered over fallen trees and around silent, dark, deathly-still pools of water. Waylond looked back at his companions. The effort it took to travel through the forest was taking its toll on Simkin. Tipping his head toward the tops of the trees, Waylond narrowed his eyes and shaded them with one paw, but he could not see the sky through the canopy.

A low creaking sound came from his right. He looked toward the noise, his entire body stiffening as he focused. The moss-covered bark at the base of a nearby tree began to ripple, undulating like a wave. The movement climbed up the trunk and inched across a low-hanging branch. As it reached the very end of the branch, its tip stretched out and met other branches on a nearby tree. The two trees entwined and the rippling moved to the next tree and the next. This continued until the surrounding trees came alive with motion and vibration.

Green tendrils burst from the branches above them, curling and extending down toward them. Waylond watched the vines drop over Simkin, whose eyes followed their descent. The creeping vine curled and uncurled before him, moving closer to his face each time it unfurled.

"Don't move," Waylond said, as he watched the vine's delicate tip stroke the fur on Simkin's muzzle and move toward to his ear, where it ran its finger over the ear's tip. The tendril then moved down toward his neck. A low squeal escaped Simkin's throat as he flashed a pleading look at Waylond. Waylond reached over his shoulder and drew his sword from its sheath. The weapon began to hum, and the vine snapped up, away from Simkin. Turning now to Waylond, it undulated toward him. Waylond raised his sword, holding it over Simkin's head. He motioned for Simkin and Wulfgar to step away from beneath the threatening creepers. Then tendrils abruptly stopped in mid-air. They seemed to inspect the sword. Gathering around it they pointed at it, and examined it, without touching it.

Scared, Simkin stood biting his claws. "Stop biting your claws, mate." Wulfgar hissed. Simkin's gaze was glued to the tendrils floating around Waylond's sword.

"All right!" Waylond shouted. "We have had just about enough!"

Stillness fell upon the forest. Where there had previously been movement and noise, now there was none. Waylond surveyed the area. The vines froze and began to retreat back to the branches. In a moment, they disappeared from sight, becoming one with the trees.

"Maybe they're gone now," Simkin offered in a whisper.

"Not likely," Wulfgar retorted. "This forest is wicked. It's not like the Forest of Sunderland."

"We're tired," Waylond said, sitting on the moist ground. "We'll rest here for a while." Simkin sat close beside him. "Here, Wulfgar, sit here."

"I'm just fine over here, numbat," Wulfgar growled.

"How long will it take before we get out of here, Waylond?" Simkin asked through chattering teeth.

"Don't dwell on that, Simkin," Waylond replied. "We'll be on our way after a short rest. We'll be out before you know it."

Waylond looked at Wulfgar. There was uncertainty in the stoat's eyes.

Chapter 14

Simkin slept for a while, and to Waylond's surprise, Wulfgar had fallen asleep as well. Waylond sighed and thought about Fergal and Bunyip. Perhaps somehow, some way, they had survived the fall. He had not expected things to turn out this way, but here he was. He had left his solitary life when Fergal walked into it. Waylond sighed again, and this time the sound felt loud in the oppressive quiet of the Styx. The only other noise was the rustle of the leaves above him. They swayed, touching each other, communicating in a language known only to the Styx. Waylond had learned to understand the Forest of Sunderland, but the whispers of these trees sounded utterly foreign. A vibration beneath him caught his attention. He moved his leg expecting to see something, but there was nothing. A shuffling to his right made him turn in Simkin's direction.

Stretching his limbs, Simkin yawned and then his eyes snapped open. He struggled to get to his feet, but the ground under him was moving.

"Don't panic, Simkin," Waylond warned.

"Oh my, oh my," Simkin fretted. He looked down at his feet. "A leaf? Is that a leaf lifting me up?"

"Yes, and it's attached to a branch," Waylond said, tilting his head, and trying to understand what he was seeing. "It looks like an arm."

Several more leaves poked up from underground. Then a round head and a pair of eyes appeared. They blinked and their long green lashes fluttered, shaking off bits of earth. Beneath the lashes the eyes were the color of a dark emerald sea. One sinewy arm held Simkin while another arm rose from the earth and reached out, its leafy fingers stroked the fur on Simkin's head. A face was now smiling at Simkin and Waylond.

"What's happening?" Wulfgar asked with alarm.

"Put Simkin down," Waylond said firmly, rising to his feet.

"Oooooo," the leaf creature exclaimed. "You are frightened for this little animal."

Simkin trembled like a shrub in a windstorm. He thrust a paw into his mouth and began to gnaw on it.

The leaf creature stood before them with Simkin still in the palm of her hand. She touched his clothes, his ears, lifted his arms and stroked his snout. She was covered with silvery leaves, and she towered over Waylond. Her legs and arms were made of twigs and vines. Turning him, the leaf creature viewed Simkin from every angle.

"What is this called?" The creature ran a fingertip across Simkin's brow. "I've seen one of these before but have never touched one. I don't know its name."

"Simkin's a bilby," Waylond answered. "And who might you be?" He looked up into the creature's green eyes. They were mischievous eyes, which sparkled with flecks of gold. Folded leaves formed thin ears on the side of her head, and tendrils of green fell in curls around her face like fine locks of hair. On her head she wore a circle of gold vines. Bright yellow leaves and red berries clung to it. It was a halo and it shone like the sun at mid-day.

"I am Chloe." She pushed a small curl of green away from her face with her free leafy hand. "I am the wood nymph, ruler of the Styx. Why are you in my realm?" She met Waylond's eyes with a cold stare, stretched herself to full height and raised her chin. She spoke, each word with firmness and without emotion. She lifted a root-like foot and took a step closer to Waylond. Clods of dirt fell to the forest floor as she moved. Her eyes wandered from his head to his feet. "No one enters my domain," she said with an empty smile.

"Well, someone did!" Wulfgar said, folding his arms across his chest. "What do ya have to say about that?"

"You have no manners, stoat," Chloe snapped. The smile left her face. She looked down at Wulfgar with scorn as her hand snapped out to seize his arm in a firm grip. "You believe you are a great leader, stoat. But I only see blades and fear. I do not see love, trust or family." She released his arm and stepped back as Wulfgar rubbed the spot on his forearm where she had held him. "You know nothing of guidance. Your control comes from the point of your sword. You have much to learn about camaraderie and family."

"Who the…"

"Wulfgar!" Waylond cut him off, moving a paw through the air. Wulfgar shut his mouth.

"You said no one enters your realm. Why not?" Waylond asked Chloe.

"Because those who enter would not find a way out," Chloe said. "What is your name?"

"I am Waylond of Acadia. That is Wulfgar, and you're holding Simkin.

"Do I know you, Waylond of Acadia?"

"I don't think so."

Chloe studied him carefully. "I think differently." She closed her eyes for a moment, then opened them to stare at Waylond. "The trees of Sunderland know you and the Styx knows you, but you have no power here." Still holding Simkin, she looked to him and smiled. She lowered him to the ground and ran her leafy hand softly across his face. "I have heard your heart, Simkin, and I know you to be sweet," Chloe said. "But you can't help anyone if you are constantly afraid, constantly fretting. You cannot achieve your goals if you are always anxious."

Startled, Simkin stared up at Chloe and then at Waylond.

"It is a terrible shame that all of you have wandered into my kingdom," Chloe said.

"If," Waylond began, "as you say, the Styx knows me, then it must also know why we are crossing through."

"Yes, the Styx knows you, but as to your mission…" Her words trailed off as she raised her head and spread out her arms to the surrounding trees. "The Styx is my magnificent realm." She studied the branches and vines above her with pride. "News of your arrival traveled quickly through our roots and branches." The boughs above her shook in response. She blinked twice, smiled, and then lowered her eyes to meet Waylond's.

"Your mission to rescue the bilby family is gallant, Waylond." The branches above her vibrated and bent slowly toward her. She closed her eyes again and lifted her arms to meet them. They wrapped around her securely, embraced her, and she smiled at them, rubbing her cheek against them. Finally, the branches loosened their grip and rose back to the canopy.

Chloe's eyes opened and she said, "You must accept your responsibilities, Waylond of Acadia. It is the only way."

Wulfgar and Simkin stared at Waylond.

"What does she mean?" Wulfgar asked.

Waylond was silent.

"Show us the way out," Wulfgar demanded of Chloe. "Ya know the way out." He unsheathed his sword and waved it in Chloe's direction. "I'll make kindling of ya, ya green goblin. Show us the way out, or else!"

"I don't have to do anything for you, miserable stoat," Chloe shot back. "Or you, Waylond of Acadia," she said, her emerald eyes flashing.

Simkin began to cry. "We'll never reach Mt. Olga now. My family is doomed. My mother, my brother..." Choked with emotion, Simkin fell to the ground, his paws covering his face.

"You *will* show us the way out," Waylond said sternly.

"And who are you to make demands of me?" she asked. "You think that every problem can be solved with a simple conversation or by simply walking away." She pointed a leafy finger at Waylond's snout. "Do you think you will know when it becomes necessary to fight? Perhaps you will hide again, deep in the forest, ignoring its call. Yes, that is what I think you will do."

"I can no longer hide, and I will know when the time comes to fight."

"Humph!" Chloe folded her twig arms together. "I think not. Sometimes peace comes at a price, and weapons must be used as intended."

Waylond stared long and hard at Chloe.

"There are many lives that depend on me," Waylond said. "When the time comes, I will recognize it."

"You will need to prove it!" With that she began to sink slowly back into the earth. The dirt rose up and wrapped about her legs. The vines caught in every branch of her form and pulled her down. "Then fight," she shouted before she disappeared into the ground. A bright flash of light filled the surrounding woodland, and Waylond lifted a paw to cover his eyes.

Chloe the Wood Nymph

Chapter 15

There was another flash of light, the ground rumbled beneath his feet, and the trees shook around him. Waylond brought his forearm up and covered his face. It only lasted a few seconds, but when Waylond opened his eyes he was standing alone. He was certain that he was in the Styx, but Wulfgar and Simkin were nowhere to be seen. He held his staff before him and scanned the area, peering through the dark twisted wood. *Where did Wulfgar and Simkin go?*

He trudged through the undergrowth, batting away great ferns and roots as he went. *I've got to find them. They must be here somewhere. How did we get separated?* He walked for a while, then stopped and leaned against an old tree to catch his breath.

"Chloe, what have you done?" he said aloud.

He pushed off the tree and started to walk through the dense undergrowth again, when a great wall of ferns rose up from the earth. He tried to walk around it, but it just grew longer, racing across the ground into the Styx as far as his eyes could see. He swung his staff at the wall but struck nothing.

"She means to do us harm," he said. "Chloe! Show yourself!"

He inspected the wall, contemplating what to do next, when the ferns came alive and began to form a creature, another numbat. Waylond's jaw dropped open. He ran a paw across his muzzle and rubbed his eyes.

"Greetings, Guardian. You do call yourself the Guardian of the Forest, don't you?" Morlund laughed.

This is madness, Waylond thought, as he brought his staff up defensively.

Knocking the staff aside with a sweep of his halberd, Morlund spoke. "No, you can't be the Guardian, can you? That was my father and you are not a fit replacement. You are fit for nothing. You are worthless."

Waylond took a step forward. The image lifted its halberd and pointed it at Waylond's throat. "Don't come near me, you useless animal," Morlund said. "You can never live up to Father's vision." Morlund's voice boomed in Waylond's ears and echoed through the forest around him.

"I, I…" Waylond stammered, trying his best to understand what he was seeing.

"You are insignificant, Waylond. Our father died for nothing." The ferns shifted and swirled before him. A great wind wound its way through the tree trunks, and the leaves overhead shrieked in agony as the gale tried to rip them from the branches.

"Morlund!" Waylond shouted at his brother over the wailing wind. "Father's death was your doing."

Morlund laughed and lifted his halberd.

Waylond swung his staff and the halberd clashed against it. He pivoted around Morlund, swinging his staff in a circle overhead. Morlund swung the halberd, and Waylond struck out, stopping its forward momentum. Morlund pulled the halberd back and swung again, but Waylond ducked as the halberd whizzed by his head. Spinning in place, he brought his staff around and struck out at Morlund's weapon once more, but his swing met only air, and he fell to the forest floor.

"It's not my fault," Waylond shouted.

The leaves shook off the limbs and rained down around him. As quickly as it had appeared, the wall and the image of his brother slipped back into the ground. Morlund was gone and the Styx was silent.

Wulfgar stood alone at the base of a large tree trunk. The tree had fallen and what remained was a splintered remnant directed toward the sky. He looked from side to side as he pulled his dagger from its sheath.

"What is going on in this wicked place?" Wulfgar shouted. "Waylond, ya ugly marsupial! Where are ya?"

There was no reply. Waylond and Simkin were nowhere in sight.

"Well, this is a fine sack of twisted snakes," he said, shaking his head. He stepped forward through the thick moss, wound his way around the tree stump and headed through the trees.

Movement in the undergrowth caught his eye. Sharp roots began to poke through the ground and rise up like spears. They laced together, forming a screen that blocked his way.

"What's happening?" He shook his head. "Who am I talking to anyway!" he yelled. Anger and frustration took hold as he stared at the thickly woven wall of roots. He walked in one direction then back the other way, spinning and turning. He couldn't get past or around the living screen. A root shot out and captured his foot. It wrapped around his ankle and yanked. He yanked back. The more he pulled the tighter the grip became.

"Why ya… ya, lousy piece of kindling!" He tried cutting it from his leg with his dagger, but it just continued to creep until he was completely entwined within the coiling roots.

"How does that feel, ya ugly stoat?"

Startled, Wulfgar tried to move his head to see where the voice was coming from, but he was completely bound, tied to the wall of twigs.

"Who is that? Come out and show yer ugly face, ya miserable varmint."

"It's me, Wulfgar. Just me," said the sneering voice—an echo of his.

A lump formed in his throat. Wulfgar couldn't speak. He was listening to himself, but where was the voice coming from. *What treachery is this?*

"Yes, this is a treacherous place," the voice answered his thoughts. "Ya are a foul one indeed. Ya think of yerself as a leader. Ya are a leader of a motley crew of scoundrels and nothin' more. Ya are a weakling. A coward."

"I'm no coward!" Wulfgar shouted. "Show yerself. I'll beat ya to an inch of yer pitiful life." He struggled to free himself, but the roots held tight.

"It's yer life that's pitiful," the voice answered. "Yer useless. Ya can't even take care of yer nephew. Ya don't even have the courage to tell him that ya care, afraid it would make ya less of a stoat, I suppose."

"Shut yer trap. I don't believe anything ya say, and when I get free, the first thing I'm gonna do is come after ya."

"Look to yerself, Wulfgar," the voice said. "Yer nothin' more than a bandit."

The roots slithered back into the ground before his eyes. He stood again before the fallen tree; its splintered trunk was unchanged. For the first time, he became aware of a cold, empty sensation in his chest. He began to walk in no particular direction.

The sound of snapping twigs came from behind. Waylond turned to see Wulfgar pushing through the underbrush and walking toward him.

"Where did you go?" Waylond asked.

"I could ask you the same question. This placed is cursed." His eyes were crazed as they scanned the surrounding woods. "This is enough for me." He scratched his head, straightened the belt at his waist, and touched his dagger nervously. "Let's get a move-on," he said. "Where's Simkin? Let's find the bilby and get out of here."

"I hear you," Waylond said.

"Yeah, that's the problem, I hear me too."

"What?"

"Ah, forget it. Let's just find Simkin and leave this place."

Waylond and Wulfgar heard whimpering from a nearby shrub. When they arrived at the source they could see Simkin cowering in terror.

"What could I do?" Simkin shouted at no one. "She told me to leave, and she told me to get help." He took in great gasps of air as he tried to speak. "My mother—my brother taken right before my eyes—and what did I do?" He pounded the ground, ripping at the moss and twigs. "I did nothing. I was too frightened to do anything."

"Simkin," Waylond said in a whisper, but Simkin continued to sob. Waylond walked to Simkin, and touched him on the shoulder. "It's all right, Simkin."

"No it's not, Waylond," Simkin cried. His eyes were wild with rage and overflowing with tears. "I can never make this right."

Waylond reached down and pulled Simkin to his feet. Simkin wiped the tears that ran down his muzzle and soaked his fur.

"We're going to find your family and the others." Waylond put his paw beneath Simkin's chin and lifted his face so he could look in his eyes. "I promise you, Simkin. It will be all right."

"What now?" Simkin asked.

"Well, if we've proven ourselves to Chloe, I expect she'll show us…"

"The way out," yelled Wulfgar, pointing to the break in the trees. A vision of blue skies and warm sunlight met them. The majestic peak of Mt. Olga was ahead. Together, they stepped out of the Styx. "Let's get out of here," he said.

Walking at a quick pace, Waylond glanced back at the forest. The leaves on the trees fluttered, and the breeze from above reached his ears with a voice he could now hear. "Go, find yourselves, accept what you are and do what you can. The more you know yourself, the stronger you will become." The Styx had spoken to him and he understood. Mt. Olga lay ahead.

Chapter 16

In the depths of Mt. Olga, a full-length mirror leaned against a rock wall. Before the gilded frame stood a young Tasmanian devil. Her soft, white fur matched the glistening white of her fangs and served to highlight her glowing pink eyes. On her head she wore a delicate crown—heavy with sparkling gems. And between the folds of her flowing pink robe, which pooled in puddles of shining satin at her feet, hints of a necklace holding a large rose-colored stone peeked out.

The rough-hewn room behind her was not particularly luxurious, but she'd done what she could. A small table, several overstuffed wing chairs, a canopied bed, and a nightstand filled the space. The chandelier's candles illuminated even the darkest corners of the room, and a cozy fireplace flickered near the chairs. In the mirror she caught the reflection of the gilded flower petals that had been painstakingly etched into the surface of her prized possession: a small black-lacquered chest. It held an immense quantity of gems and jewelry fit only for a queen, which, she supposed, she was, in a way.

The gems were gifts meant to keep her happy. But her happiness came at a price. She was as much a prisoner in this mountain as the enslaved bilbies, numbats, wombats, and other miserable creatures that mined it. They'd been forced to dig the rooms, passages, and tunnels that made up this labyrinthine underground prison. Shafts carved through the rock with their blood and sweat released acrid smoke into the sky from the fires, which were always kept burning in the great forge, fired by the volcano's hot lava.

The beauty of clouds floating across the sky and the warmth of the sun were a distant memory. She'd been abandoned as an infant at the base of the mountain. If Morlund hadn't found her and taken her into what had then been only a series of small caves, she would have succumbed to the elements. He'd been her savior. And ever since, he'd struck fear into her heart. For every gem his slaves dug up for her, Morlund had a dozen blades forged from the mountain's rich ore deposits. For her, nothing remained except a dazzling collection of stones. Otherwise, she had nothing but captivity and a sickly fear that she could barely contain.

A small sound in the hall caused her ears to prick up. She looked toward the chamber's entryway as Morlund crossed the threshold of the open door.

"Ah...Nedra. You sparkle like the jewels themselves!"

She shied away.

"Morlund! How dare you come here unannounced," she snarled, over her shoulder.

"The door was open. We haven't spoken for days." He stared at her back. "I just thought…"

"Don't do it again, Morlund," she interrupted. "You have been good to me, but don't think that means you can just walk in here any time you like."

Her warning was clear. Nevertheless, he took a step closer to her. Reaching out one paw, he placed it on her shoulder and turned her to look at him. "You look beautiful this evening. The pink of the rose stone matches your eyes and nose." He reached for the crystal and took it into his paw, turning it over, examining it.

"My gem setter just completed this necklace today." She smiled, raising her head to meet his gaze. She took the crystal from his paw and walked to the fireplace where she sat before it. She could sense a flickering of almost insane cruelty in him, and she pushed her fear deep down. She would not allow him to see it. There was something about him, something from his past that he didn't share. She accepted this and felt that it was best not to know. Nevertheless, a shiver crept up her spine like a spider walking across a web searching for prey.

"Any news?" she asked. "Have you found what you've been looking for? I think you've forged enough weapons."

He strode across the stone floor and sat in the chair next to her. "I will do what I must to find the right combination. In the meantime, I must prepare. I must be ready for the battle that is certain to come." Flames from the fire reflected in his eyes, and Nedra could see the determination there.

"I don't understand," Nedra said.

"It's simple, Nedra. The mixture of ores must be perfect or the sword will not accept the crystal."

"And the battle?"

"Not all battles are fought with swords, Nedra."

"Morlund. " She cocked her head to one side and fluttered her eyelashes at him. "Can I see it?"

He raised a paw to the leather pouch that hung around his neck. Carefully, he pulled the pouch from beneath his shirt. When he opened it and removed the crystal it filled the room with a green aura that touched every corner of the chamber. Even the candlelight took on a green cast and Nedra's fur glowed a sickly green in the light of the sparkling crystal. She reached out to touch it.

"May I wear it?" She licked her lips, and her paw opened and closed, anticipating that he just might drop the crystal into it.

Morlund pulled it back, placed it in the pouch and dropped the pouch beneath his shirt. "No, Nedra," he said.

She retracted her paw and frowned at the numbat. "But you said you would let me wear it."

"Not today." He leapt to his feet and walked toward the bed. "Why do you keep asking me?" He swung a powerful paw, hitting the black box on the nightstand. It crashed to the floor, its contents spilling out onto the dirt. "What I'm doing is more important than these trinkets." He glared at Nedra, and she pressed herself against the back of the chair. "More bilby slaves will be found. We will open a new tunnel…dig for more ore, forge more swords…"

"You need slaves for farming as well," Nedra interrupted. "You need them to take care of the fields at the base of the mountain. How else will you feed them?"

"Their needs are secondary to mine," he hissed.

The sound of footsteps in the tunnel outside Nedra's chamber caught their attention. Stepping into the passageway, Nedra and Morlund could see a flickering light coming toward them. Around a bend in the tunnel, a tall, thin Tasmanian devil stepped into view. Three smaller devils and a dragon lizard carried a badly burned bilby on a stretcher. Flitch, the skulking thylacine confidante and henchman of Morlund, bounded beside the group on all fours. His mouth hung open and saliva dripped off his knifelike canines.

Nedra could not stand the dog. He was stronger than any thylacine she had ever known and more terrifying. His muscles rippled as he strode toward them. His yellow eyes pierced her to the core. He was mangy and cared for nothing other than Morlund, and she could not understand how he put up with the disgusting creature.

"What happened?" Morlund demanded of Flitch.

"Nothing much." Flitch shrugged. He sat back on his haunches, ran a paw across his mouth, and wiped the drool away. "We had a small accident near the forge."

"What kind of accident?" Nedra asked.

"A pot of molten gold spilled," Flitch said. He raised a paw to his mouth and began picking his teeth with a sharp claw. "A number of bilbies were cooked, um, I mean burned." Flitch licked his chops and snickered under his breath.

"What do you mean, 'a number? How many?" Morlund demanded.

"Only five." This time it was the thin Tasmanian devil who spoke up. He smirked at Nedra. "I don't think they's gonna make it." He smiled, revealing a toothless grin. "But we have taken in the inhabitants of a nearby village," he said. "We can always find more of those stinkin' rats."

Morlund narrowed his eyes and looked down the dark tunnel.

"What is it, Morlund?" Nedra asked, peering down the passageway. "Do you see something?"

"No, but I feel something." His paw rose to his chest, covering the leather pouch beneath his shirt. "He is coming. Well, well, well. Now it begins."

He headed down the tunnel toward the center of the mountain and the forge. As he passed by Flitch, he grabbed the thylacine by the ear and tugged. "Follow me, dog!" The thylacine whimpered and fell into step behind the powerful numbat. "We've got work to do."

Flitch

Chapter 17

Bede stood before the forge in the center of Mt. Olga. Heat from the bubbling molten lava filled the cavern. Sweat rolled off the tip of his nose and dripped to the floor, where it hissed and evaporated into a puff of steam. The bottoms of his shoes were worn, and he could feel the heat from the stone floor penetrate them to the soles of his feet. All around him, bilbies, wombats, numbats, and dibblers ran to and fro, working to dig the ore for Morlund's weapons. Some were forging weapons for Morlund's army of dragon lizards and Tasmanian devils. Others were working in an adjacent room creating jewelry for Nedra.

The creation of the sword, that one sword, was his responsibility. Flames shot from the lava, sending smoke to the rock ceiling of the cave where it escaped through vents tunneled into the mountain. He held a pickaxe in his paws, walked to the wall where he had made progress before, and broke off more chunks of rock. A pile of rocks was collecting at his feet; much of it sparkled with ore containing precious minerals that he hadn't known existed before he was dragged in chains to this awful place.

At least Simkin escaped, he thought. The knowledge that his brother was free gave their mother hope. She'd been locked in a horrible, cramped cage since their arrival. He looked up. Hanging from the wall was Morlund's halberd. The mighty weapon was used to frighten everyone within the central forge. Bede shook his head sadly. *There must be a way*, he thought.

Every night he would plan a new escape, but he knew it was fruitless. He looked around at the despondent faces of his fellow creatures. They'd given up. Morlund held all their families' hostage. They were fed just what was necessary to keep them alive. How could they even think of escaping? If any worker tried to flee, their family would be slaughtered. Morlund was ruthless. He cared for nothing except the resources found in the dark depths of the mountain.

Bede felt a paw on his shoulder. It was Rufus, the grey mouse-like dibbler. The dust and small chips of rock from within the cave covered his coat and dulled the spots on his coarse, speckled fur. His round black eyes were dull and lifeless. In the sunlight, they would shine. Here they reflected only fear and flames.

The dibbler's sharp nose twitched as he spoke. "Bede, have you a leftover crumb of bread from last night's meal? Me mother's not well, and I think maybe a bit more tuck would help."

"Sure, Rufus." Bede reached into his pocket and pulled out a moldy piece of bread. "It's not much, but it's yours, or your mother's, that is."

"Ah, thank you, Bede. You're a saint sent from the Guardian himself." The dibbler reached out a paw and touched Bede's arm. "Tell me what I can do to repay you."

"No, no." Bede smiled and shook his head. "Giving is all we got right now, Rufus. Consider it a gift, okay?" He looked down at Rufus' foot. "How's that foot of yours? Is it feeling better?"

"Better, much better. Thanks for asking." He lifted it and wiggled it around for Bede to see. "Like new it is, since that rubbing you gave it. That's all it needed. Just a quick massage, and it's almost like new."

The chains they used to drag the dibblers and bilbies into Mt. Olga were too heavy for the small creatures, and many feet and ankles were injured as a result.

"Thanks so much for the bread." He looked at Bede. "One day we're gonna do something great, Bede. You and me, we're gonna do something great." He glanced around the cave. Flames leapt from the forge and smoke passed between the two small marsupials. Rufus waved a puff of smoke away from his face. "We'll get out of here, Bede. We will. Then we'll do something great and I can give you a gift too." He limped away, swallowed by a cloud of smoke.

"Well, from your mouth to the ears of the Guardian," Bede said to no one.

Thunderous footsteps echoed through the cave, and the sound of rattling swords accompanied them. Morlund stepped through a cloud of smoke. He stood before Bede, Flitch at his side. His yellow eyes drove into Bede like a drill, and his white fangs reflected the red flames of the forge. Morlund struck fear into the heart of every bilby and dibbler beneath the mountain.

"Where is the newest sword?" Morlund demanded of Bede. His eyes narrowed and his voice echoed throughout the cave. A foul wind crawled up the walls and slithered out of the surrounding tunnels.

"It's in the cooling room, Sire." Bede took a step back to escape Morlund's glare. But there was no getting away. Morlund bent down, grabbed Bede by his long ears and lifted him off the ground. "This time it had better work, bilby, or else."

"I told you that I know nothing of weapons. I forged farm tools, nothing more."

Morlund threw Bede across the cave. He hit the rock wall and fell to the ground. In two giant strides the numbat stood over Bede as he tried to scramble to his feet.

"Well, it's just your bad luck that you happen to be a blacksmith then, isn't it?" Drawing his sword from its sheath, Morland held the point to Bede's throat. "I have given you the opportunity to learn a new skill. I want no excuses from you," he snarled. "Now show me what you've forged."

"Yes, Sire." Bede hurried toward the cooling room with Morlund at his heels.

On a stone slab near the center of the room lay a sword. Two dibblers were shining the hilt and smoothing the opening where the crystal would rest. Morlund swung a paw, connecting with one of the dibblers who fell to the floor at Bede's feet.

"Get out of my way," he demanded.

"There's no need to push them around, Sire," Bede said. "They've worked hard to help me forge this sword, just like the dozens of swords that came before it."

"Shut up, bilby!" Morlund shouted. "You talk too much, and defending these miserable rodents does you no good."

Morlund reached into his shirt and pulled out the leather pouch out. Turning it over, he dropped the green crystal into his paw and stared at Bede. Bede could feel those eyes piercing his chest, and his heart throbbed with dread.

"We still have a number of mixtures to try, Sire," Bede offered. "I mean if this sword is not suitable for the stone..."

A growl from Morlund cut off the bilby. Morlund studied the sword. Placing a paw on the blade, he bent to put the crystal in the hilt. As soon as the crystal and sword came together, the sword began to hum, and Bede's eyebrows rose in surprise and hope. The humming continued as he stood over the sword, watching it with hope and trepidation. Rays of light shot out from the crystal. They bounced off the cave walls and reflected in Morlund's eyes. Bede held his breath, thinking that perhaps this just might be it. Then it happened, like so many times before. The green rays became black, while the hum of the sword became a high-pitched scream. Starting low, the scream rose in volume, and Bede pulled his ears down against his head. The sword's shriek was deafening. As the black rays imploded against the hilt of the sword, tendrils slithered from the crystal and crept down the blade and up to the hilt. Where they touched the silver, the blade turned from a dull grey to an inky black. The screech reached a fever pitch, sending cracks from the hilt to the tip of the sword. With a final piercing shriek, the sword shattered on the stone slab and fell into a million dark shards leaving the green crystal intact. Its aura was now gone, leaving the crystal dull and inert as though the effort to fit into the hilt had taken away its life.

Morlund threw back his head and roared. The entire mountain began to tremble. Dirt and rocks loosened and fell all around. He stared at Bede, his paws balled into fists, and then he closed his eyes. Black mist leaked out of cracks in the rock walls forming long-legged spiders that crawled toward Bede. Quickly, Bede scurried backward until he hit the edge of the forge. Thrusting a paw out, he held onto the forge itself. The spiders came closer.

One of them touched his foot and began crawling up his pants' leg. Others crept along the forge, marching in a steady cadence in his direction. Bede gasped, gripped the rock wall, and winced. "You have one more chance, you miserable rodent." Morlund yelled in Bede's face. At the wave of Morlund's paw, the spiders disappeared. "Build a sword that will accept the crystal! If you can't build it then your mother is dead." Morlund bared his teeth. Bede could feel his hot fetid breath against his face. He curled into himself, trying to make himself smaller. "Do you understand me, rodent?"

"Yes, Sire," came Bede's response. "We can try again. Please don't hurt my mother!"

"I leave that up to you," Morlund said, and walked out of the cave.

Bede fell back against the forge and sank to the dirt floor. "How will we ever get out of here?" he sobbed.

"I'm here, Bede," Rufus said softly, pulling at his friend. "We have work to do."

Bede rose to his feet, shook his head and looked Rufus straight in the eyes.

"You're right, Rufus. There is still work to do, and we will get out of here. I promise you."

Bede & Rufus at the Forge

Chapter 18

It was dark. Fergal floated along with her eyes tight. It was like being on a cloud, a cloud in heaven. She didn't want to open her eyes, afraid that the feeling would end. It did anyway, with a thump. Her paw automatically reached out as she was lifted and rolled onto a hard surface. Her eyes opened. In the dim light, she watched as a rubbery nose came out of the water and webbed feet lifted another body and deposited it next to her.

"Bunyip!" Fergal crawled over to him. His eyes were still closed and it was too dark to tell if he was hurt. "Bunyip, can you hear me?" She shook him, he groaned, and then rolled over onto his back.

"He was okay when we found both of you clinging to a branch," said a voice.

In the faint light, Fergal saw two creatures climb out of the river and scramble next to her.

"Yeah, we don't know where you came from," said a second voice.

Fergal peered into the darkness. "Who are you? Did you bring us here?" she asked.

"Yes, we did!" said the two voices. The voices were high pitched and every word gurgled like water bubbling around rocks.

"Oh, my." Fergal rubbed her eyes. She recalled falling, and when she hit the water she had struggled to the surface, her paw still tightly clasped in Bunyip's. "I barely remember what happened." She peered toward the sound of the voices. "You're duckbilled platypuses," she said.

"Yes, we are," said one. "And when you arrived on the rapids, we picked you up and swam here with you on our backs." His bill flapped the words out and his little black eyes sparkled in the dim light. "We happened to be at the right place at the right time."

"That's right," said his companion. "The river slows here underground, and when we saw you floating along wrapped around that tree limb, we simply picked you up and brought you here." He slapped a webbed foot on the stone and shook water from his shiny coat.

"And where is here?" Fergal asked as she looked around.

"You're in a cave under the mountain," said one platypus.

"Where am I?" Bunyip said groggily, as he coughed up water.

"Bunyip. You're all right!" Fergal helped Bunyip to his feet.

Fergal and Bunyip, saved by the Platypuses

"I'm wet!" Bunyip complained. He bent over and coughed, spitting up water. "What do you mean by 'under the mountain?'"

Fergal's eyes had adjusted to the dark and she could now make out the rock walls of the cave. Stalactites sparkled overhead, dripping water into the slow moving river, which disappeared into the darkness. Could they be under Mt. Olga, the same mountain Waylond had talked about?

"Bunyip?"

"Yes?"

"Do you think this is where Simkin's family might be?"

The two platypuses began waddling toward the river.

"Hey wait, you two!" Fergal shouted after them. "Are you leaving us...? Is this Mt. Olga?" She no sooner got the words out than the two slid into the river and disappeared. "Well, I guess they are." She shook herself and water droplets flew in every direction. She tried to wring water from her jacket and pants. "Bunyip," she said as she ran her paws over her jacket, "I don't know about you, but I'm not getting wet again. I was hoping the platypuses would help us find a way out, but that's not going to happen. They left us."

"That's fine with me. I'm used to being abandoned anyway," Bunyip said. "I don't need some damp platypuses to tell me where to go or what to do."

"You're not abandoned," Fergal said. "We didn't even know their names, and they saved us. It's not always about you, Bunyip."

The Platypuses

"What would you know anyway," Bunyip said. "You probably grew up in a sweet little village, in a sweet little house and had a sweet little family."

"My brothers always made fun of me," she said, placing her paw on her chest.

"Well, at least you had brothers and a family. My family left me alone in the forest." Bunyip glared at Fergal. "Can you imagine how it feels growing up and never knowing who your mother and father were?"

Fergal opened her mouth to say something and then thought better of it.

"Ah, forget it," Bunyip barked. "Let's get out of here."

"Okay," Fergal said. Changing the subject, she added, "If we are beneath Mt. Olga, Waylond will be showing up here. After all, this is where we were headed. We just happened to arrive first," Fergal said with a cheeky grin, trying her best to lighten the conversation. "Remember what he said? His brother is here, and the crystal he needs to complete his sword is here."

"I remember, but that's not the only thing beneath Mt. Olga," Bunyip continued. "I told you and Waylond that there's an army of Tasmanian devils here. Do you remember that?" Bunyip asked as he poked Fergal's shoulder. He grabbed Fergal's arm and leaned in real close to her face. "There's not much you and I can do. This is Waylond's problem, not ours."

"That's selfish, Bunyip," Fergal said. With a jerk, she shook off his paw. "I thought you might have realized by now that we can help you and that Waylond can help you. As a matter of fact, he saved your life, and you're just going to walk away? Do nothing?" She pointed a claw at him. "You're not as dangerous or tough as you make yourself out to be."

"You don't know anything about me, Fergal."

"You're right, I don't. But I do know that Simkin's family might be here somewhere, and the green crystal might be here too." Fergal started to walk away, then paused a second to look back at Bunyip. "I can understand that you're hurting, Bunyip. Maybe you're angry because you never had a family, but we could be your family. We care about you. Waylond cares." She shook her fist in frustration. "Why do you think I fell? For me? I tried to save you." Bunyip stood silently before her. "I'm going to find that crystal, and I'm going to get it to Waylond so he can complete the sword." She hammered her fist at the air. "I'm gonna help 'cause Waylond needs me. If you don't want to come with me, fine."

Fergal watched as Bunyip stopped looking at her and began lifting his face to stare up over her head. She followed his gaze. Two huge paws held a spear above her. She turned slowly and backpeddled toward Bunyip.

"Lookie, Monti. Lookie here!" A tall, thin Tasmanian devil with only one canine stood over Fergal and Bunyip. His short, fat companion stood next to him. The short one, Monti, had a mangled mess of a left ear—as if it had been bitten off. "Wow! Wonder where they came from?" the thin one continued. "They don't look like much."

"What, what's that you said?" Monti asked in a loud squeaky voice. "We'll get in touch?"

"No stupid, I said THEY DON'T LOOK LIKE MUCH?"

"What, what's that you said?" Monti asked in a loud squeaky voice. "We'll get in touch?"

"No stupid, I said THEY DON'T LOOK LIKE MUCH?"

"Well, maybe so, but they don't look like much to me," said Monti.

Jiemba groaned, jabbed his spear into the dirt and bent down to his companion. Getting real close to the one ear that was intact, he shouted, "WHAT SHOULD WE DO WITH THEM?"

"How the heck should I know?" Monti's paw swung up and pushed at Jiemba's snout. "Stop yelling, I'm right here. I'm not deaf."

Jiemba took a step back from his cohort and looked down at Fergal. "So say's he." He pointed at Monti's ear and grinned, showing Fergal his lone tooth.

"Maybe we should take them to Nedra, Jiemba," Monti yelled. "She's always complaining she's alone. What do you think, mate?"

"Why would we do that?" Jiemba replied. "We should bring them to Morlund to work in the mines."

"Yeah, but there ain't no pines here," Monti said. "We're under the mountain, remember?"

"Not PINES, I said MINES, MINES!" Jiemba yelled. "We're supposed to take any creatures we find to…" Jiemba let out an exasperated sigh. "You heard Monti. We'll be taking ya to Nedra. Don't give us any problems."

"Good," Monti said with a smile. "I hear ya loud and clear!"

"That'll be the day," Jiemba said with a smirk.

"I always said it, Jiemba," Monti said. "You got a really fine mind. Really fine." Both devils began to laugh. Their laughter echoed off the walls of the cavern. Monti took a length of rope from a pack on his back and Jiemba lowered his spear at the two wet companions.

Fergal grabbed Bunyip by the paw. There was no place to run. The two devils blocked their way. *I guess we're gonna meet Nedra*, Fergal said to herself.

Chapter 19

Monti tied their paws together, while Jiemba prodded and poked them with his spear. Fergal and Bunyip would be going nowhere without pulling each other along.

"Get a move on," Jiemba said, as he thrust the point of his weapon into Fergal's spine.

"Stop it!" she yelled over her shoulder. "We're moving. No need to poke us."

"Oh, dear," laughed Jiemba. "Better say our prayers to the Guardian. This one's tough, and I'll bet she's got friends in high places." The comment seemed to amuse both devils and they began to giggle.

"Oh, yeah," Monti said, holding his belly. "Ooooo…we gotta be real careful 'cause the Guardian is gonna get us!"

"What Guardian?" Jiemba sniggered.

"What's that you say? Did I hear you say "What Guardian?"" Monti asked, still laughing. "That's a good question. He's nowheres!" Jiemba slapped his companion across the back, sending him flying forward into Bunyip.

"Off of me, you big moron!" Bunyip snarled.

"Ah, we has another feisty one here," Monti said.

As they continued down the torch-lit tunnel, their shadows crept across the rock walls and their footsteps echoed around them. Fergal could smell something burning. It was the stench of sulfur and metal. She watched Bunyip scan every inch of the passageway as they walked along. *He's looking for a way out,* she thought. *We've got to figure out where the crystal is kept and get it to Waylond.*

A few yards ahead a door opened and a rectangular pool of light flowed out into the passageway before them. The devils grabbed Bunyip and Fergal by the collars and held them in place.

"This concludes our tunnel tour," Jiemba snorted.

"What's it for? What do ya mean 'what's it for'?"

"I said TUNNEL TOUR, ya deaf lout."

"Tunnel tour," Monti repeated. He grabbed his friend's arm and laughed in his face. "That was a good one. 'Tunnel tour.' We should give more tours, don't ya…?"

"Shut up, you worthless idiot," Nedra said as she stepped into the tunnel and stood before them. Fergal couldn't help but stare. "What are you doing? Why have you brought these creatures here?"

They were deep beneath the mountain, and it was hard for Fergal to believe that such an animal could live here. Nedra was a beautiful Tasmanian devil, as white as freshly fallen snow. Her nose, eyes, and inner ears were an intense pink. She was dressed in a blue satin gown that fell to the floor, and a circle of gold, encrusted with different colored stones, sat on her head like a crown. A huge green crystal in a gold filigree case hung from a chain around her neck, and a gold bracelet surrounded her wrist. Her pink eyes flashed in anger at the two devils, and they lowered their heads, rubbed their muzzles and scratched their ears anxiously.

"We found these two by the river," Jiemba said, offering a slight smile.

"Yes, we thought you might like them as pets, or maybe…" Monti hesitated. His eyes narrowed, examining the crystal around Nedra's neck. "Hey, isn't that Mor…"

"Be quiet!" Nedra cut him short.

"Sorry, Ladyship, I thought it might be…"

"No one cares what you think!" Nedra waved her hand in front of Jiemba's face. "You're putting your ugly snout where it doesn't belong. It's none of your business."

Jiemba cast a suspicious look toward Monti and then back at the crystal.

Nedra moved toward Fergal and Bunyip. She reached out a paw and examined Fergal. "I've never seen one like you. What is it?" she said to Jiemba.

"It's a quoll, Lady," he said. "Me mother told me about them. They's got lots of white spots, but you can hardly see this one's…"

"Enough," Nedra interrupted. "Get them inside." With a shove from the devils, Fergal and Bunyip found themselves on the rug inside Nedra's chamber. "You two get lost," Nedra growled at the two devils. "I don't want to see you back here. Oh, and don't tell Morlund about these two creatures." She squinted at Bunyip and Fergal. "He's got enough on his mind with that sword he's trying to build." She stared at Fergal. "I don't think he'll ever be able to find what he's looking for," she said to no one in particular. Her paw wrapped protectively around the green crystal.

Fergal chanced a quick glimpse at Bunyip. The recognition was clear on his face, and she touched his paw. *She knows Morlund. That's got to be the green crystal Waylond needs.* Fergal looked at it and considered what she might do. Waylond would be so proud of her.

Nedra paced back and forth, wringing her paws nervously. Fergal watched her carefully. She thought she even saw the white devil trembling. *She's afraid*, Fergal thought. Bunyip was right. There was a lot to be frightened of in this place. Even Nedra didn't seem comfortable.

"Why are you two still standing there?" Nedra shouted at Monti and Jiemba. "Didn't I tell you to get out!"

Jiemba glanced over his shoulder one last time at Nedra as they raced out.

"Close the door!" Nedra yelled at him, and the door slammed shut.

Nedra circled Bunyip and Fergal slowly, touching their ears, stroking their fur and fiddling with their clothes. Fergal took a few moments to gaze around Nedra's room. It was a cozy place, with chairs in front of the fireplace and a large bed. Yet, she couldn't imagine living down here and never seeing the sun. She looked at Nedra again and found herself staring at the necklace.

"That's beautiful," Fergal ventured, pointing at the green crystal.

Nedra lifted her paw and touched it. "Oh, this," she said. "It's very special."

"Do you think you could untie us?" Bunyip said in an annoyed tone.

Nedra glared at Bunyip.

"Mind your manners, Bunyip." Fergal elbowed him as she spoke. "We are Nedra's guests. Isn't that right?" Fergal smiled her sweetest smile at the white devil.

"Why, yes, that's right," Nedra said with a smirk. "Didn't your mother teach you any manners?" she said to Bunyip.

"I don't have no mother," he replied.

"Well, I don't..." Nedra stopped short. Then she walked to the door, pulled a key from a pocket on her gown and locked it. "I'll untie you," she said, dropping the key into a pocket on her robe. "But don't get any ideas." She shook a claw at them. "It's dangerous in the caves, and you'll get picked up and spend the rest of your pitiful lives with the other slaves." She then untied the rope binding them together. "Do we understand each other?"

"Yes, Ma'am," said Fergal, rubbing her wrists. "I don't have any ideas, other than to dry out a bit, and I'm hungry. I think Bunyip is too." Fergal turned to Bunyip. "Right, Bunyip?"

Reluctantly, Bunyip nodded. "Yes, that's it. We're wet, tired and hungry."

"Well, we can fix that," Nedra said. She walked to a small cabinet, opened it, and pulled out a covered bowl. "Why don't you take off your jackets and spread them out by the fire so they will dry out. Then you can sit here." She placed her paw on the back of a wing chair by the fire. "What are your names?"

"I'm Fergal, and this is Bunyip."

Fergal and Bunyip removed their wet coats, laid them on the hearth, and climbed into one of the chairs together. Nedra put the bowl on the table and sat in the chair across from them. The bowl was filled with the largest acorns Fergal had ever seen.

"Acorns!" Fergal exclaimed. She pulled the acorn her mother had given her from her pocket and held it out to Nedra. "I have an acorn. See! My mother gave it to me. She painted it. It was a gift."

Nedra leaned forward and stared at the acorn in Fergal's paw. "Why, that's beautiful. What a wonderful gift." Nedra reached her paw out to take the acorn, but Fergal pulled it back. Nedra's pink eyes flared, and a small hissing sound slipped from her lips. Fergal gazed down at the painted acorn she held in her paw and hesitantly held it out again. Nedra's anger was replaced with a smile. "You can...can hold it if you like," Fergal said.

"Thank you." A softness came over Nedra's face. Her shoulders relaxed as she gently took the acorn from Fergal and turned it over so she could see the painting. "Your mother is talented." She handed it back to Fergal. "She must love you very much." After what seemed to be a long time, Nedra said, "When you've had enough to eat, you can settle down on my bed and rest."

"That's very generous of you, Ma'am, but we've got to go right away," Bunyip said. "Our family will be missing us. Won't they, Fergal?" Bunyip nodded urgently at Fergal.

"Ah…yes," Fergal said. "They will be missing us."

"I'm sorry," Nedra smiled. "But you're not going anywhere anytime soon." Nedra's eyes flashed with anger, and she pushed the bowl of acorns toward them. "Now eat!"

After Fergal and Bunyip had their fill, Nedra voiced her next command. "It's time to sleep," she said. Grabbing them both by the collar, she pushed them to the bed. They curled up together and watched as Nedra walked back to her chair and glared at them. Soon she closed her eyes.

"She's dangerous," Bunyip hissed in a whisper.

"I realize that," Fergal agreed. "We need to think of a plan to steal the crystal and get out of here."

"So how are we going to do that?" Bunyip said with a muffled squeal. At the sound, Nedra stirred and she glared at them through squinted eyes. Fergal and Bunyip froze and remained silent until Nedra's eyes closed again.

"We'll have to be still until she's asleep," Fergal said. "Then we'll make our move."

Bunyip nodded and they settled in to wait.

Chapter 20

Fergal blinked. How long had she been asleep? The unexpected trip downriver had exhausted her and Bunyip too, who was sleeping alongside her.

"So you know something of the crystal?"

Fergal's head whipped around. Nedra leaned out from behind the wing of her chair and eyed her. Fergal shook her head. The white devil's shining pink eyes captivated her.

"No," Fergal whispered.

"Come now. I heard you talking about it in your sleep," Nedra said. "We can be good friends, but you must be honest with me." She patted the arm of the chair near to hers, inviting Fergal to sit.

Fergal hopped off the bed and walked to the chair, her eyes never leaving Nedra's. "To be perfectly honest, Bunyip and I would like to get out of here." She climbed into the chair.

"Why do you want to leave? You just got here, and we're just getting to know each other." Nedra's voice was soft, almost comforting, but Fergal wasn't sure that she was sincere.

"You have a nice little place here, but I would think you would become tired of looking at rock walls and dirt floors. Don't *you* want to leave?" Fergal asked. She saw surprise in Nedra's eyes. "It must be awful living down here with all this smoke and never seeing the sun."

"Why would I want to leave?" Nedra shrugged.

"This place frightens me. It makes me nervous and upset," Fergal said. "I think you're nervous too."

Nedra hesitated. "Morlund does everything for me." She frowned, leaned back into her chair and stared blankly into the flames of the fireplace. Then Fergal realized why Nedra had looked nervous before. Nedra wasn't in charge. She was as much a prisoner here as they were.

"You do want to leave, don't you?" Fergal was beginning to understand. "It must be awful down here…"

"What makes you say that?" Nedra asked with a sneer. "I have everything I need."

"You don't have everything. You don't have friends, and you seem rather lonely," Fergal said. "Why would you be so interested in keeping us a secret?"

"It's got nothing to do with friendship," Nedra snapped. "If I don't keep you a secret, you two may end up dead." Nedra's voice dropped. "You have no idea what you have fallen into."

"I know that you are not happy. Have you ever left this place?" Fergal asked. "Have you ever sat in the sun alongside a river, watching the frogs jump from one rock to another? Have you ever seen the wallabies hopping through the grass searching for seeds and fruits?" Fergal moved her paw up and down, imitating the frogs she had seen living along the Gabbling. "Have you ever felt the joy, that comes from gathering your own food and drink? Have you ever had a hug?"

Nedra's paw moved to her necklace and she stared, examining Fergal. "I don't need those things," she said flatly.

"Oh, but you do!" Fergal said. "Everyone does. It's what makes life so interesting—so wonderful. It's part of the challenge and thrill of being alive." Fergal's excitement at sharing the joys of life grew with every word she spoke. Soon the words were flowing faster than the Gabbling itself. "Sometimes I can't do everything on my own, and sometimes I'm not so sure of myself, but I'm learning that there are things I *can* do. Things I never dreamed I could do." Fergal laughed. "That's when a good friend comes in handy. I'm sorry, Lady, but it makes me happy to think of these things. They remind me of my mother and what she taught me." Fergal wrung her paws and looked up at Nedra. "I miss her. The river keeps taking me to places I never thought I would go...so far away from everything I have ever known." She took the acorn out of her pocket and looked at it. Bringing it to her chest, she said, "I have a new friend who cares about me. He cares about everyone."

Nedra rose from her chair and walked to the fireplace. "And who might that be?" she asked, staring into the flames.

"The Guardian. He will come for me." Fergal dropped to the floor and crossed to stand beside Nedra. "He can help you too…if you want." Fergal reached out a paw and took Nedra's in hers. Nedra cleared her throat and blinked down at Fergal.

"The Guardian?" Nedra asked. "I have heard about the Guardian from Morlund, and none of what I have heard is good. In any case, I can't accept his help." Nedra backed away from Fergal.

"Yes you can. Don't be afraid. We can leave together, but we need the crystal."

Nedra's paw flew up and grabbed the crystal around her neck. She backed against the wall of her chamber and Fergal saw the fear rise in her eyes.

"You have to give it to me, Lady."

"And what do you think you are going to do with it?" Nedra barked. "It doesn't belong to you!"

"It belongs to Waylond. He is the Guardian of the Forest." Fergal straightened her back and gathered all her courage. "If you don't give it to me, he will come. He'll come to get it."

With a crash, the door to the chamber fell to the floor and Morlund stood in the threshold, filling it, blotting out the light from the tunnel. Morlund stared at Nedra, then looked from Fergal to Bunyip, who had fallen off the bed with a thump.

"What do you think you are doing, Nedra?" he roared. "Who are these rodents?"

"They were lost in the tunnels and two of your devils brought them to me —to entertain me," Nedra said calmly.

"And I guess you thought it best not to tell me about them."

"I saw no reason to tell you. I..."

Morlund strode over to Fergal. Gripping her by the scruff of the neck, he lifted her off the ground and held her directly in front of his snout. "Who are you, and what are you doing here?"

Fergal squirmed and the more she did the tighter his grasp became.

"Who are you?" he repeated as he shook Fergal. She closed her eyes. Then, with a growl, he threw her on the bed. "Guards!" Monti and Jiemba appeared in the doorway. "Take these two to the prisons. They will work at the forge. We can always use more help." He glared at Fergal with a malicious grin. "So you think the Guardian will come," he said. "Yes, I think he'll come to save your sorry hide. Perhaps he will bring what I need."

Fergal looked at Nedra. She did not move; she would not help. Fergal knew this. Nedra was frightened and would protect herself. Fergal felt sad for her. She had no life of her own and was incapable of doing anything. *I will have to wait for Waylond, but I need the crystal.*

"You can't do this to us!" Bunyip's paws balled into fists. "Let us go." He grabbed Fergal off the bed and pulled her to him.

"I don't think so, young stoat," Morlund said with a snarl. "You are now my property. I rule under this mountain." Morlund bent toward Bunyip. "I decide if you live or die." Curling his upper lip, baring his sharp white fangs, he stared at Fergal and Bunyip with murderous yellow eyes.

"Leave them alone," Nedra said. "They can do no harm."

"Do no harm, you say?" Morlund grabbed Nedra by the throat. "You think you can keep things from me, Nedra, but you can't. Even behind closed doors, I know what you are doing and what you are saying." He pointed at Fergal and Bunyip. "They know my brother, they know about the crystal, and you say they can do no harm?" He tightened his grip and Nedra grimaced in pain. "I'll make sure they do no harm!"

"Let me go," Nedra gasped. "You're hurting me."

"You're lucky I don't do more to you." Morlund pushed her away and yanked on the chain around her neck as she fell to the floor. The chain broke, and Morlund held it. "You have betrayed me, Nedra. I have been good to you. Taken care of you! I should never have allowed you to wear this." He crushed the gold case around the crystal with his paw, and dropped the chain to the floor. "Take them!" he pointed at Bunyip and Fergal. Both guards stepped forward to seize them. "No!" Morlund pointed to Jiemba. "You stay here and guard the doorway." Jiemba stepped away while Monti grabbed Bunyip and Fergal by the collars. He wiped the dirt floor with them as he dragged them into the tunnel. Fergal took one last look at Nedra. She saw shame and sorrow in the white devil's eyes.

"I'll be back for you, Nedra," Morlund barked. "Don't worry. I'll be back for you." He dropped the crystal into the pouch around his neck and followed close behind as Fergal and Bunyip were hauled toward the prisons beneath Mt. Olga.

Chapter 21

Dirt and stones hit Fergal in the face as she and Bunyip were dragged through the tunnels. Bunyip struggled beside her, but the grip of the devil was too strong and he could not break free.

"Stop yer kicking and thrashing, ya mangy rodent." Monti jerked Bunyip who hit his head against the rock wall.

"Ow!" said Bunyip.

"That's what ya get," Monti said.

Fergal could feel the temperature in the air rise. They had reached the forge at the center of the volcano. She could see a number of creatures running to and fro, adding fuel to the fire and helping to create all kinds of weapons. Swords, daggers, spears, and shields hung from the walls.

They entered another tunnel, which led to a dimly lit cavern. Cages filled with animals of all sizes were lined up against the walls.

"This concludes our tunnel tour," Monti snickered. "That's so funny. I really like that—tunnel tour! It makes it sound so interesting." He thrust Fergal and Bunyip into a cage and shut the door with a clang. "Maybe not that interesting," he laughed as he fastened a chain around the bars and secured it with an iron lock. Hanging the key at his waist, he peered in at Fergal and Bunyip. "There ya go, my fine little rodents. The next tunnel tour begins…never! Enjoy your stay." He walked away, laughing loudly. "I slay meself – I'm so funny!"

Fergal looked at Bunyip. "Now what?"

The blank look on Bunyip's face was all the answer Fergal needed. She let out a deep sigh and leaned back into a corner of the cage.

"Well, dear," a small voice said, "unless you have a skill of some kind, more than likely you'll be in that cage for a while."

Fergal and Bunyip glanced into the next cage. The bilby they saw there was wearing a blue tattered shirt and skirt. She looked thin and frail but offered them a smile. Fergal gripped the bars of her cage and looked across at the bilby.

"Hello, my name is Fergal," she said, peeking through the bars. "And this is Bunyip." Fergal waved a paw in Bunyip's direction. "There are so many here," she said, as she scanned the cave. Cages covered every wall, some stacked on top of each other. Many of the creatures were quietly talking to one another, reaching out of their cages to stroke and comfort their companions through the bars below or next to them. Fergal shook her head.

"Yes, it is awful." The bilby reached for Fergal's paw and Fergal took it in hers. "My name is Mirindah."

"How long have you been here?" Bunyip asked.

"Oh, dear, I've simply lost track of time." Mirindah twitched her nose and looked at Fergal thoughtfully. "My son Bede knows. I'm sure he can tell us."

"When can we talk to him?" Fergal asked.

"I don't know, dear. He's trying to forge a special sword for that nasty numbat," she sighed. "He is being forced to do it." She wrung her paws over and over again, then wiped a tear from her eye.

"It's all right, Mirindah," Fergal said. She rubbed Mirindah's paw gently. "You're going to make yourself more upset. I can see how troubled you—"

It was like an electric shock had shot through her. "Wait a minute," Fergal said. "You said your son's name is Bede. Right?" Fergal leaned against the bars of the cage, pushing her nose between them. "By any chance, do you have a son named Simkin?"

"Why, yes I do!"

"We know Simkin!" Bunyip said, leaping up.

"Oh, my." Mirindah's eyes opened wide and she squeezed Fergal's paws in hers. "Is he all right? Is my boy all right?"

"Yes, he's fine," Fergal said. "No worries."

"Thank the Guardian. My boy is safe." Mirindah smiled.

The sound of boots echoed through the cavern and a devil wearing a dagger at his side entered the cave. He took his dagger from its sheath and ran it across the bars of the cages as he walked around the room. The rattling sound it made caused all the prisoners to move to the back of their cages, where they held their paws over their ears.

"Stop with the chit-chat, ya filthy rats." The devil licked his lips and leaned in toward one of the cages, peering in at the prisoners. "I will be guarding the likes of you guys for the evening, and I'm not as soft as Monti, the deaf idiot. So don't give me a hard time, and everything will go smoothly for ya." He laughed, then knelt down to look at Fergal and Bunyip. "You guys are new. We hope you enjoy your stay. We have chips and water on the dinner menu." He stopped for a moment and gazed at the roof of the cave with a reflective look on his face. "Oh, wait," he said, looking down at Fergal with a mischievous grin, "we're fresh out of chips. Oh what a terrible shame. Tsk, tsk, tsk. Guess you'll have to do with just water."

Fergal stood and placed her paws on her hips. "It's so easy for you to be tough when we're sitting in here and you're out there," she said.

"I should smash you good and hard." The devil reached into the cage and tried to grab Fergal, but she stepped back and pressed herself against the far corner. Grunting, he pulled his arm back and removed a dagger from his belt. Then he bent to open the cage with his key and said, "I'll teach you..." A loud whack made his eyes open wide, and his jaw became slack. He fell in a heap at the front of the cage. When Fergal looked up, she saw Nedra with a club in her paws standing over the unconscious devil.

"That was easier than I thought it would be," Nedra said with a grin.

There was instantaneous commotion in the room as the creatures started chattering all at once. Nedra picked up the guard's keys and stepped to the center of the room.

"You must all be quiet and listen to my every word," she whispered. "We do not want to attract any attention. Once I open the cages, we must stay close together, and we will all get out of here."

"How did you…I mean the guard…at your door…" Fergal was stunned at what Nedra had done.

"When he wasn't looking, I clobbered him over the head with my box of jewels. That stupid box was finally put to good use. Anyway," Nedra continued, "I had to show you that I do value friendship too and, you're right, I need to get out of here as much as you do."

Fergal and Bunyip nodded. "Getting out sounds good to us," Fergal grinned. "And you're quite regal without the jewels and the crown."

Nedra smiled and looked around the room. "Getting everyone out of this cave will be easy," she said, as she began opening the other cages. "It's getting them out of the mountain that really worries me."

Chapter 22

Waylond, Wulfgar and Simkin, quickened their steps now that the Styx lay behind them, and the Forest of Sunderland, which grew thick at the base of Mt. Olga, was ahead. Waylond stopped a moment to watch the black smoke rise from the volcano's peak. The smoke swirled up in twists and coils, choking the clouds drifting by. The winds had picked up, and the leaves on the trees trembled and shook. Waylond held his palm up toward the canopy. *The Forest is in a rage.* With that last thought, he rushed headlong into the trees with Wulfgar and Simkin close behind.

The events of the past few days troubled Waylond, and the loss of Fergal and Bunyip haunted him. He was concerned that the Forest's anger might be focused on him. Its stiff wind blew fiercely and sliced through the treetops like a knife. Branches bent toward the ground in waves. Pounding the earth, they sent tornadoes of leaves and twigs in furious circles around rocks and tree trunks.

For so long, he had not accepted that he was the Guardian. He did not take up his responsibilities to the Forest and its creatures. *Did I take too much time? Am I too late?* The trees strained, creaked and groaned, but they held firm to the earth, refusing to give in to their own fury. As he ran, Waylond watched the roots rise from the soil. Like great brown limbs, they entwined, drawing strength from each other.

What was causing this natural ferocity? Was the Forest angry that its creatures were being held captive beneath the mountain? He wasn't sure, but he was now committed to whatever lay before him. He knew he would face his brother soon. He would do everything in his power to stop him and free everyone beneath the mountain. The voices of the Guardians and the words they had spoken at Windjana Gorge were fresh in his mind. Verdigris was right. He needed to leave the past behind and take on the mantle, accept the power of the Forest as it was foretold.

Then the fury of the Forest stopped.

"What's happening?" Simkin cried.

Waylond took a few steps toward a giant gum tree and placed a paw against its trunk. Heat from the bark flowed into his paw and through his body. He closed his eyes and concentrated. Something was moving across the Forest's floor, skulking, slinking toward them in slow deliberate surges.

"What now?" Wulfgar grumbled. "More trouble and trickery from the Forest?"

Waylond ignored Wulfgar and glanced at the treetops.

"Something is coming," Waylond said. He peered through the trees toward the mountain and then focused on the thick underbrush. The foliage blurred. Ripples of heat rose off it, and the green leaves lost their color. They shriveled into themselves. Absorbed by the branches and twigs from which they had once grown, they disappeared entirely. The underbrush thinned, leaving the three friends without its protection. The base of the mountain came clearly into view.

"Find cover, Wulfgar. Take Simkin and hide!"

"Who are ya to order me around, numbat?" Wulfgar said, then wilted slightly under Waylond's stare. "Okay, well I'll stuff him somewhere, but only to get the bilby out of me way."

A fallen tree was the best shelter the Forest offered. Wulfgar grabbed Simkin by the arm and dragged him to the hollow log and pushed him inside it. He covered the opening with dead branches and twigs to protect him. "Stay put, ya puny rodent," he shouted at Simkin as he ran to join Waylond.

"Simkin is safe, tucked inside a log," Wulfgar said. "It's you and me, Guardian. Now tell me, what's happening, and what I can do?"

Waylond said nothing. Instead he responded by pointing toward the base of Mt. Olga. "There!" he said.

A thunderous noise echoed off the mountain. Nearby rocks burst open and four snakes squeezed out, forming a circle around Waylond and Wulfgar. Their oily black scales were as dark as midnight. A crest of red plates ran from between their eyes down their backs. They hissed malevolently, their forked tongues tasted the air and their red eyes glared.

A fifth massive serpent rose directly in front of Waylond and Wulfgar. The dirt behind the snake began to boil and a black cloud of smoke materialized from the earth. Within the cloud was an image of Morlund. His eyes blazed with anger. In his left paw, he held Fergal and Bunyip. In his right paw, his massive halberd pointed at Waylond.

Wulfgar gasped. "They're alive, Waylond. It's your miserable brother? He has them!"

Morlund threw back his head and laughed, a malicious light shone in his eyes. "Yes, I do believe I have found something you misplaced. I am guessing they have some importance to you. If you want them both to stay alive, you may wish to leave the sword with a little friend of mine." Morlund nodded at the serpent standing before him. The snake stared directly at Waylond. Its black body was as thick as Waylond's, its maw wide enough to swallow him whole. Its tongue flicked. Its fangs dripped with venom. The rest of its body coiled and writhed with an obscene eagerness.

"Morlund, let them go," Waylond yelled, taking a step forward. The beast struck out, snapping at Waylond while separating him from his brother's smoky form. "Let them go! They're innocent," Waylond yelled.

"There is no such thing!" Morlund said. "We both know this." His image began to dissipate into the air. "Don't be foolish, brother." He waved his arm and the images of Fergal and Bunyip disappeared. "The Forest will accept me when I grasp the sword in my paw and place the crystal in its hilt."

The nearby trees of the Forest shook, and the ground rumbled. Morlund lifted the halberd above his head, and the trees bent away from him. The wind whipped, howling in anger. The gusts pounded Waylond and Wulfgar, but they stood fast against it.

"You will obey me, brother!" Morlund swung his halberd and pointed it at Waylond. "Do as I say, or the two young ones will die..."

With a wave of Morlund's paw, the serpent lashed out at Waylond, and the smaller snakes surrounding them began to close in. Waylond stepped aside to avoid the giant snake's venomous fangs. While the surrounding snakes moved toward Wulfgar, Waylond tried to fight off the serpent that swayed over his head.

"Give the sword to the serpent," Morlund demanded one last time before the smoky cloud and his form within it disappeared.

The snakes were slithering around them, readying themselves to strike. Dirt and debris flew, as Waylond quickly sidestepped each of the serpent's powerful lunges. Nearby, the roots from a tree sprung out of the earth, wrapped around a snake, strangled it, and dragged it down into the ground. Wulfgar fought alongside Waylond, swinging his sword, and slicing two of the snakes. One snake slithered up behind Wulfgar and grabbed him by the ankle, dragging him through the undergrowth toward the bottomless hole in the earth from which it sprang. Screaming, his arms flailed as he grasped at passing trees and bushes in an effort to free himself from the snake's hold. He slashed at the snake with his sword, but the creature continued to drag him along. Glancing at Wulfgar, Waylond waved a paw at a tree over Wulfgar's head.

"Wulfgar! Grab hold of that branch."

Directly above Wulfgar a branch from a nearby tree bent toward him. He reached up with a free paw while using his sword to continue slashing at the snake. The tree bent back, pulling Wulfgar off the ground. When he kicked his foot free, the snake lashed out and bit him. Howling in pain, Wulfgar hacked the air with his sword. An errant swing connected with the snake, cutting off its head, and its body dropped into the opening in the earth. Wulfgar released his hold on the tree branch and fell to the ground a few feet from the bottomless pit, which the snake seemed intent on making his grave.

Waylond struck out again and again at the giant serpent, yet it lunged from one side to the other, mirroring his moves in an attempt to take the sword from his paw. Grimacing with his effort, Waylond swung his sword with final deadly precision. The head of the serpent flew from its body. The creature's tail continued to coil and twist on the ground until at last it lay still.

His chest heaving from exertion, Waylond knelt beside Wulfgar.

"I'll be all right. No worries," Wulfgar said through clenched teeth, his paw wrapped around his swelling ankle.

Simkin scurried out of his hiding place, and examined Wulfgar's wound. "It looks bad," he said.

"You're going to stay here," Waylond said as he took a container from his vest. "Here, Simkin. Apply this once now and then again before night falls." He handed the tin to Simkin, then rose to his feet. He took hold his staff in one paw and held his sword out with the other. He gazed at the opening where the green crystal needed to be placed. *It's only a weapon until it is joined with the crystal,* he thought. *I need to accept my responsibility.*

"What are you going to do?" Simkin asked. He glanced up at Waylond, his eyes full of worry and concern. "Where are you going? You can't go on without us."

"He's right, ya know," Wulfgar said, rubbing his ankle.

"Wulfgar, you're in no condition to come with me." Waylond sheathed his sword on his back as he spoke and held his staff tightly in his paw. "I'll be going on my own from here. I must face Morlund alone."

Chapter 23

Fergal stood next to Nedra, who had led the entire group to a small cave that opened onto the river. Bunyip tapped Fergal on the arm, and she turned to him.

"What is it?" she asked.

"It looks like we're gonna get wet again," he said with a grin.

"Ugh!" Fergal let out a sigh. "Nedra, is this the only way out?"

"No, it's not," she replied, "but I believe it's the shortest. There's a path alongside the river that leads out."

The large group of animals consisted mostly of females with babes in arms or children at their sides.

"What about the men folk?" one dibbler asked. The baby she held squirmed, and she rocked on her feet to sooth it. "We don't want to leave without them. Is there no way we can reach them?"

Before Nedra could reply the ground beneath their feet began to vibrate.

"What's happening?" Fergal said, staring at Bunyip. Stones and dirt fell from above their heads. "Watch out!" she shouted, as a large stalactite shook loose and fell from the ceiling. With a crash, it shattered into a million pieces right in front of them, blocking their path. Exiting by way of the river would now be impossible.

"Back up," Nedra yelled. The cave wall behind them cracked and split open.

"I don't understand it," Fergal said. "What do we do now? We can't stay here. It's too dangerous." She and Bunyip had come so far and the thought of never getting out was frightening her. She still needed to find the crystal. *There must be a way*, she thought.

"Come on, everyone!" Nedra corralled the group back toward the passageway they had come from. "There are many tunnels under this mountain. We'll find another one that will lead us out." They all walked back, but the ground continued to tremble and shake.

"Look, Fergal!" Bunyip said, pointing at the tunnel wall. A crack had formed and was opening. A thin root was poking its way through the crack. Then an opening appeared farther down the tunnel where another root slithered out. Over their heads and along the tunnel walls, more fissures and cracks opened, and more roots wormed their way through. They were weaving in and out of the breaks in the rock wall at a slow but steady rate.

"There's more," a young bilby yelled. "Over there!"

Fergal looked in the direction the bilby was pointing. She watched as hundreds of roots grew from the rock walls and wove their way toward the center of the mountain. "The trees are coming in." She took a step toward a root that was just poking through the wall. "What are they doing?"

"Don't go near it, Fergal!" Bunyip said. "It will strangle you like the gympie-gympie tried to strangle me."

"No, I don't think so." She took another step forward and stretched out her arm, extending a claw to touch the small growing root. She glanced over her shoulder at Bunyip and Nedra. They were trembling, as was every other creature in the crowd. "It's all right," Fergal assured them. "I think it's the Forest." With that, she touched the stem and it wound itself lightly around her wrist. Startled, she took a quick step back, but green shiny leaves burst forth from it. Then the root continued up her arm. Fergal looked at Nedra, Bunyip and the others. "It's the Forest," she repeated excitedly. At her shoulder the root slithered up to her ears and circled her head where white arum lilies blossomed. The root fell back, leaving the flowery crown on Fergal.

"Well," Bunyip said, his eyes wide with wonder. "I don't think I have ever seen you smile like that!"

"Yes, she's beautiful." Nedra agreed. "And I don't think we need to fear what's happening here. Fergal's crown seems to be a sign."

"I'm not afraid," Fergal said. "The Forest has come to help us. I think Waylond is here too. I feel it." The roots continued to multiply, forming a lattice against the rock and dirt walls. The lattice buttressed the dirt and rocks over their heads before it grew toward the center of the mountain. As they moved the roots grew larger, thicker, and stronger, and the fissures they created in the mountain grew wider.

The small group was protected from the rumbling and shaking right where they stood.

"I guess we'll stay here," Nedra said, as she took stock of the surrounding stems and tubers. "The roots have certainly bolstered the dirt walls. Who knows what will happen farther up the tunnel." As though the mountain had heard her, there came a great noise. The sound of grinding and crushing rocks under a tremendous strain and weight filled their ears. The women and children gathered close together and sat in the center of the tunnel, protected by the surrounding network of roots. Nedra took Fergal's paw.

"Are you all right, Nedra?" Fergal asked.

"I'm fine, Fergal," she said softly, "I'm better than I've ever been." With that Nedra got up and walked from one bilby to the next dibbler, to the next and so on, checking with them and stroking their heads to sooth and comfort them.

"At first I thought she was mean," Fergal said to Bunyip.

"Yes, so did I," Bunyip said, shaking his head. "Strange how sometimes you don't understand someone the first time you meet them."

Fergal considered what Bunyip said and was silent for a moment. "I misjudged you...at first. I'm sorry, Bunyip. I didn't understand everything you had been through. I didn't realize you had no mother or father, and no brothers or sisters. I guess even brothers and sisters who tease and taunt you would be better than none at all."

Bunyip cleared his throat, hung his head and fiddled with the buttons on his jacket. "I know," he said in a whisper, barely loud enough for Fergal to hear him. "I'm sorry too, Fergal. I behaved badly at times."

Fergal reached out and wrapped her arm around his shoulder. "No worries. I'll be your family, Bunyip," she said. "We can be family for each other, and if I ever find my way home, you're welcome to come live with us."

"Thanks, Fergal."

Chapter 24

Waylond glanced back at Simkin. He was bent over Wulfgar, applying the cream to his wound. Wulfgar scowled at Simkin's touch. *The pain will keep Wulfgar from walking on that foot,* he thought.

Waylond headed toward the mountain. As he ran, he thought about his father and mother, both of whom he had lost. His brother was lost to him as well, which was, in some ways, even more painful than the loss of his parents. He wondered if he had handled things right or if his attempts to hide from his past had finally caught up to him. Both his fate and that of countless others now teetered on the edge of a blade. He had made a conscious choice to abandon his responsibility to the Forest. The price of that decision was being paid in black smoke billowing from the mountain, in families torn apart, and in the suffering of his people. His brother had called him unworthy and a coward. There had been disgust in those words, and Waylond had allowed himself to believe they were true. The wounds those words inflicted did not heal, and the words could not be taken back. *Yet, there is always forgiveness,* he thought, *even though the words cannot be erased from my mind.*

He scrambled along the base of the mountain, looking for an opening at the volcano's foundation. Stopping for a moment, he watched smoke from the crater drift up and darken the afternoon sky. The smoke brought a shower of stones and sparks raining down around him. *My brother's anger is shaking the very core of Sunderland and this volcanic mountain is going to explode.* A growl rose in his throat and he released it, roaring toward the mountaintop. The sound echoed off the mountainside. In response, a stiff wind rolled forcefully from the Forest, and the trees bowed toward him. He swung his staff in a circular motion above his head, then pointed it toward the ground. The roots from the Forest's trees twisted and drilled into the rock at his feet, opening a fissure. He walked forward into the darkness.

The cavern was dark, but the roots of the trees continued to plow through the rock and stone and opened a tunnel before him. He hadn't gone far when he heard voices. As the roots split the rock, it separated. He saw a small group of creatures cowering behind a pure white Tasmanian devil.

"It's Waylond!" Fergal shouted as she ran to meet him. Waylond dropped his staff and gathered the tiny quoll up into his arms. "I'm so happy to see you, Waylond."

"Fergal, I thought I would never see you again," Waylond said, hugging her. "I thought I lost you." He felt his heart burst with joy. *I found her. She's safe.*

"Don't forget me!" Bunyip said.

"Bunyip!" Waylond smiled as he put Fergal on her feet. "How did you two get here?"

"It was just like the last time," Fergal giggled. "The Gabbling brought us. We didn't have much of a choice." She grinned and ran a paw over Waylond's snout. "Boy, am I glad you're here."

"Me too, my young friend," Waylond said.

"So, you're Waylond?" Nedra said. "You must be Morlund's brother. I was warned about you. He said you were trying to steal his birthright." She examined Waylond carefully. "You don't look like the twisted and ugly numbat that Morlund described to me." She shook her head in disbelief. "I trusted him. Now I wonder how much truth there was in anything he told me."

"Truth and trust are earned," Waylond said. "It takes an open mind and heart to recognize that. I think you have both." Her eyes could not hide her surprise and awe. "As for me," Waylond continued, "I have come to accept my own truth."

Waylond smiled down at Fergal. Her faith in him brightened the darkness within the cave and made Waylond feel loved and strong. His purpose was now clear in his mind and he would not falter.

"I told you he would come," Fergal said, excitement rippling through her voice. "Now all we have to do is get the crystal. Right, Waylond?"

"We? Who said we're going to get anything?" Waylond asked.

"But, I know where it is," Fergal said.

"Yeah, it's around that other numbat's neck," Bunyip added with a smirk. "How are we gonna get it?"

Nedra reached out and laid a paw on Bunyip's head. "Bunyip's right, you know," she said, looking at Waylond. "Your brother is wearing it."

"We'll help you get it," Fergal said, placing her arm around Bunyip's shoulder. He nodded his agreement. It was obvious to Waylond that his two small friends were ready to stand beside him.

"All right," Waylond agreed. "But I want you both to stand behind me and do as I say." He pointed a claw at them. "Is that understood?"

"Yes!" Fergal and Bunyip said as they raised their paws in salute.

"How far are we from the center of this mountain?" Waylond asked Nedra.

"It's not too far. Go directly through this tunnel," Nedra said, pointing down the passageway. "You will reach a cavern. Two other tunnels open into that cavern. Take the steep tunnel heading down. It will lead to the forge at the center of the mountain. You will feel the heat as you get closer," she explained.

The mountain rumbled.

"I'm afraid this volcano is not going to hold together much longer," Nedra said.

"I have to agree," said Waylond.

"You should find Morlund at the forge," Nedra said. "He's been trying to create a sword for that *green rock*. Many innocent creatures have died trying to build the sword for him."

"It's not possible for him to forge the sword," Waylond said. "There's only one sword the crystal will accept." He reached his paw over his head and removed his sword from its sheath. "This is the one sword."

The crowd behind Nedra craned their necks to look at it. The blade seemed to glow in the dim light of the cavern, and the area brightened as Waylond held the sword before him. Then, in one swift motion, he replaced it in its sheath.

"I don't know what your plan is," Nedra said, "but I must get these mothers and babes to safety."

"What about the men, our brothers?" a kowari from the crowd stepped forward to ask.

"The Forest and I will bring them to safety. I promise," Waylond said with a nod.

"And us too," added Fergal.

"Take the group out the way I came in," Waylond said to Nedra. "You'll be safe in the Forest. It will protect you."

"Be careful," Nedra said. She reached out and touched Waylond's arm. "Your brother is full of hatred and anger. I never understood it, but there is something sad there as well." She shook her head and dropped her paw to her side. "He never spoke of it, but something has taken his heart. I pity him."

Chapter 25

With long strides, Waylond walked deep into the center of Mt. Olga; Fergal and Bunyip close at his heels. The ground shook beneath their feet, and dirt and rocks fell from the tunnel walls. Waylond knew there wasn't much time, but on the way, the roots of the Forest moved with determination along the passageways with him. The tubers thrust themselves into the rock and then emerged from it farther along the passageway. Every time the roots emerged, leaves burst from the tubers covering the dirt walls with flashes of green, bringing life to the dreariness, while buttressing the rock walls.

They reached a point where the tunnel opened up into a small cavern, just as Nedra had described. From the opening Waylond could see two tunnels. Leaning against the rock wall, he glanced down at Fergal and Bunyip.

"Be still. I hear something," Waylond whispered.

Fergal scratched an ear and turned her head toward the open area of the tunnel. "I hear it too," she said.

"Someone's coming," Bunyip added.

"Yes, but it's more than one someone, Bunyip," Waylond warned. He peered around the edge of the tunnel into the cavern. A troop of armored dragon lizards and devils moved at a quick pace from one of the tunnels across the open area heading into another passageway. Their chests were covered with steel-clad plates, and their forked tongues licked the air as they ran. Some carried spears, axes and shields, while others had swords sheathed at their sides. The sound of their movement clattered, echoing off the tunnel walls.

When the last of the group disappeared into the tunnel, Waylond stepped out and looked down the passageway. As the final lizard disappeared around a curve, he waved his paw before the entrance. The Forest's roots burst from the rocks and began growing, weaving a net across the opening. The crisscrossed roots became tighter, thicker, and denser until the opening became an impregnable wall of tubers.

"They won't be coming back this way," Waylond said. "The Forest has made certain of that." He glanced down at Fergal and Bunyip. "Let's go!" They ran into the tunnel from which the horde of lizards had emerged.

The heat intensified as they moved deeper into the mountain. The trembling and shaking became more forceful the closer they approached the center. Finally, Waylond entered the inner most cavern. The forge in the middle of the room was a giant well of bubbling molten metal surrounded by a low rock wall. Flames shot from the forge to the stone ceiling high above their heads. An emaciated bilby stood at an anvil alongside the forge. He raised a hammer over his head. On the anvil, ready for his hammer's strike, lay a sword. The bilby stopped in mid swing and turned his face toward Waylond. Dropping his arm and he placed the hammer on the anvil.

"We have waited for your arrival, Guardian," the bilby said, with a small, sad smile. "Why have you taken so long?"

"I'm sorry," Waylond replied.

A commotion in a nearby room caught Waylond's attention, and he stepped in front of Fergal and Bunyip to shield them. A group of frail and exhausted forest creatures entered the forge from an adjoining cavern. Stunned looks were frozen on their faces. They carried blacksmith's tools in their paws, tattered clothes hung from their skeletal frames, and their sunken eyes told of many days of hard labor with little food to sustain them. One of them stepped forward. "What's happening here, Bede?" he asked.

"The end of this cruelty," Bede replied.

"Bede," Waylond said, touching him. "Take these men and boys back up the tunnel. The Forest has created a new exit. Bring everyone through it to safety. Hurry." The mountain quaked and they braced themselves as the earth moved under their feet and rocks fell from the ceiling.

Mt. Olga was preparing to erupt, and shook with fury. Then, from its depths came the sound of pounding feet. Fergal and Bunyip ran to a crack in the rock wall, squeezed in and hid themselves. Bede hustled the group to the tunnel and waited until the last bilby, dibbler and kowari scampered into it. Moments later, terrified screams came from the passageway, and Bede glanced back at Waylond, but it was too late. Morlund appeared from the tunnel with a squirming kowari in each paw. He threw the kowaries to the ground and they scampered back down the tunnel. He bent down and grabbed Bede by the throat.

"Where do you think you're going, bilby?" With his face against Bede's, Morlund curled his upper lip and rested his canines against Bede's snout.

"Let him go, Morlund," Waylond snarled.

Morlund's eyes burned into Waylond's. "Since you've asked so nicely..." Morlund mocked. He thrust his paw out, holding Bede at arm's length in front of him. Bede's limp body hung from Morlund's paw, his eyes squeezed shut. Morlund released his grip and Bede fell to the ground, where Morlund kicked him toward Waylond's feet. He struck the stone base of the forge and lay there motionless. Waylond glanced at Bede and knelt down. When he was satisfied that Bede was still alive, Waylond placed his staff beside the unconscious bilby. "This is my gift to you, Bede." He stood and turned his attention to his brother.

Opening his arms, Waylond took a step toward Morlund. "We are family, Morlund," he said. "There is no longer any need for this hatred to continue. Your anger has shaken the very foundations of Sunderland, and you have used the Forest's innocent creatures cruelly, but we can end this."

"Innocent!" Morlund flung out his arm and pointed a claw at Waylond. "Unlike you! You are guilty!" He took the halberd that hung on the wall behind him. Spinning it, he walked toward

Waylond. The point of the mighty weapon stopped at Waylond's throat.

Waylond looked down at the weapon. "We are both guilty, Morlund," he said. "Guilty of carelessness in choosing our words and recklessness in what we have done, but we can change that."

"Nothing can be changed. The past has been forged in the fires of our minds. There is no amount of water that can quench the flames. I have thought about this meeting from the day I left our home in Acadia. I knew we could not escape this fate."

Morlund raised a paw and swiped it across his snout and up over an ear. For a moment, Waylond hoped his brother would relent, and things would be as they were before, when their mother and father were alive, when they were young, when they loved and protected one another. But those times were long gone, and as much as Waylond wanted it to be different, the damage had been done. He yearned for brotherly affection from Morlund, but they could not take back their words or their actions. Even if he had come forward sooner, had left his shed in the Forest of Acadia sooner, even that thought was useless to him now. It didn't matter anymore. The finality of it all struck him like a dagger to the heart. He felt a pain he had not felt since he saw his mother drop beneath the surface of the Gabbling, or his father fall at the hands of his brother.

"I wish it could be different, Brother," Morlund said in a hush. He lowered his halberd, looked down and shook his head. "Decisions have been made. I have seen this battle in my dreams." The flames from the forge behind Waylond reflected in Morlund's eyes. With his halberd brandished before him, he shouted, "Draw your sword, brother. We must end this here and now!"

"You are right about one thing, Morlund," Waylond said. "The Forest has always been a witness to our lives, and it will be our witness once more. I wish it could be different, but I see now that we are both damaged. You felt betrayed, and I was insecure, reluctant to take on my responsibilities. Perhaps, somehow, some good can come from this."

In one swift motion, Waylond reached over his back and pulled the sword from its sheath. Morlund swung his halberd over his head and their weapons met with a clash. Tongues of fire rose up from the forge, and swirls of molten metal churned at its center. Waves of power rippled out from each of the angry brothers like breakers on the surface of the Gabbling.

Morlund slashed at his brother, the blade of his halberd barely missing Waylond's ear. The reflection of the flames from the forge flashed off their weapons as the powerful brothers fought. With his sword held across his chest, Waylond ran at Morlund and pushed him against the wall of the cave, pinning him to it.

"Where is your honor?" Waylond shouted at his brother.

Morlund's narrowed eyes glared into Waylond's. "I left it in Acadia in that old gum tree you burned to the ground."

Reflected in his sword, Waylond caught sight of Bede scurrying across the cavern with the staff in his paw. *Run, Bede, run!* In a flash, the bilby disappeared into the tunnel.

Waylond released Morlund, and their weapons clashed once more. The power of Waylond's thrust sent Morlund reeling back, striking the wall of the cave. Morlund's arms flung open and he let out a groan as his halberd flew out of reach. Weaponless, Morlund hauled himself up and ran at his brother, landing a punch to the side of Waylond's head. Waylond staggered backward. Hitting the forge with tremendous force, Waylond crumpled to the floor.

Chapter 26

Morlund bent to pick up his halberd, but roots sprouted from the earth and took hold of it, pinning it to the floor. He let out a blood-curdling call. At his command, thick, black fog rose from the dirt at his feet. The fog solidified into black eyeless snakes that squirmed toward the Forest's roots. Curling his lip, Morlund raised his fists, and strode, without a weapon, toward his brother. Waylond flung his sword away and moved forward to meet him.

The sword landed in front of Fergal and Bunyip, who were still hunkered down in a small crack in the cave wall. Fergal reached out for it, but it was too far away. She grabbed Bunyip by the shoulders and shook him. "The sword, Bunyip, the sword," she said, pointing at it. "We have to get it."

Bunyip stretched out, but he couldn't reach it either.

"I'm crawling out there," Fergal said.

"Are you crazy?" Bunyip screeched. "Look at those black things. They're everywhere."

Bunyip was right. The black smoke that came from the earth under Morlund's feet had thickened, then divided. Hundreds of snake-like creatures were creeping and slithering everywhere, choking every root in the cavern.

"It's not too far away. I have to try," Fergal said. "I'll crawl out, and you hold on to my ankle and pull me back. If I stand up, those black snakes will see me, or Morlund will."

"Okay. I'll pull you back!"

Fergal began crawling out of their hiding place. She pressed herself to the ground, trying to stay out of sight of the black creatures and Morlund. A bit at a time, she wiggled to where the sword lay. Its empty hilt and blade glittered in the light of the many small fires, which now burned on the floor around the forge. Roots hissed and shriveled, turning black from the flames, and withered back into the ground where new ones would sprout up. With one great effort, Fergal lunged out and wrapped her paw around the sword's hilt.

"Pull me back!" Fergal shouted over her shoulder to Bunyip. "Pull me back!" A black snake rose from the earth and twisted around the blade of the sword and tried to yank it away from her. "It's got the sword, Bunyip. Pull harder!" Fergal was sure that the leg Bunyip had hold of would become longer than the other from his pulling, but the black creature would not let go and neither would she. When it seemed she could not hold on any longer, a stem erupted from the ground and grabbed the black snake, wrenching it away from the blade. With a jerk, she was dragged along the floor, the blade tightly clutched in her paw.

"We got it," Bunyip said. "Now what?"

Trembling with fear and excitement, Fergal pressed herself into the crevice beside Bunyip. She brushed the dirt from her snout, looked at the sword and then toward the forge. Morlund and Waylond were still in the throes of hand-to-hand combat. Waylond was kneeling on his brother's chest as Morlund's paws were clenched around Waylond's throat. Waylond pointed a claw toward the wall, and a huge root exploded from it. The root rushed along the ground and twisted itself around Morlund's neck. It pulled him along the dirt floor and up the stone wall where it pinned him firmly to the rocks. With a wave of his paw, Morlund sent a black snake to twist around the root, enfolding and choking it. The tuber withered and fell to the ground, setting Morlund free. Waylond raised a paw, and at his command another root erupted from the rock wall, but a dark snake exploded from beneath the dirt, twisted itself around the root, and strangled it.

Morlund's sinister laugh bounced off the walls, and Fergal and Bunyip covered their ears with their paws. Waylond grimaced, preparing to call forth another root, but a black snake erupted from the ceiling above the forge. It dropped down behind Waylond and wrapped itself around Waylond's ankles. Lifting him off the ground, the eyeless snake pulled him upward and held him upside down over the bubbling cauldron of the forge.

"What do we do?" Fergal asked.

"Fergal!" Bunyip shouted. "He sees us."

Fergal saw Morlund walking toward them. She pushed Bunyip deep into the crevice before he had time to protest. Then she grabbed the sword by the hilt and began to drag it toward the forge.

"What are you doing?" Bunyip yelled. "He'll get the sword."

"Stay there, Bunyip," she yelled. "I'm bringing the sword to Waylond!"

Waylond hung over the forge, while flames licked at his ears. Twisting toward Morlund, his paw punched the air. A bolt of lightning sizzled across the room and struck his brother in the chest. It slammed him into the rock wall, and roots erupted from the rock wrapping themselves around Morlund's arms and legs. Two more roots burst from the rock and tied themselves around his neck. Snarling, he shifted his head back and forth in a useless effort to free himself. Another two roots burst from the wall at his waist and encircled him. Now Morlund was securely fastened to the wall of the cavern. It was then, as Morlund struggled to free himself, that a small, thin root grew from the larger one around Morlund's neck. It wiggled down to the leather strap holding the pouch with the crystal. This small root twisted and pulled at the strap until, with a powerful jerk, the pouch was sent sailing across the room, where it landed in the dirt.

Fergal was on the move toward the forge, determined to get the sword to Waylond, when she saw the pouch fall to the ground. "Grab it, Bunyip!" she shouted.

Bunyip dashed out from the crevice and took hold of the pouch. A horrifying howl came from Morlund as he thrashed to free himself from the roots. In response to Morlund's fury, the flames from the forge surged upward.

Waylond curled himself up and held on to the body of the black worm-like tendril holding him. It was enough to keep him clear of the flames, but his paw slipped and he dropped closer to the molten metal. He began swinging back and forth above the flames. In one swift movement, he pulled his dagger from his belt, twisted up and sliced the wraith. Waylond fell, almost clearing the forge, but his head hit the rim and he lay unconscious in the dirt.

Darting between the dirt and rocks that fell all around him, Bunyip dropped to the ground at Fergal's feet, the pouch in his paw, his chest heaving. Morlund let out another deafening roar, and the mountain trembled with his anger.

"Give me the pouch!" Fergal said, thrusting a paw to Bunyip. He handed it to her and she pulled the crystal out. Holding it in her paws, for a split second she was stunned by its beauty. It was the color of the Forest, and it sparkled like nothing she had ever seen before. It sent out rays of green light throughout the cavern, bathing everything in its glow.

"Put it in the sword!" Bunyip urged.

"No!" Morlund shouted. He closed his eyes tightly, and a hot wind blew in from the tunnels. Cracks appeared in the stone all around them, and a small break appeared in the wall near the forge. Molten lava seeped out from the fissure, creating a twisted thread of flame that moved along the dirt. A stone fell from the ceiling, hitting Fergal in the back. Her paw hit the ground and the crystal fell out. It rolled up to the edge of the forge and came to rest there. Bunyip helped Fergal to her feet.

With the sword in his paw, Bunyip helped Fergal stumble toward the crystal. As they neared it, Morlund let out another deafening roar. The walls split again, and the sound of cracking and rupturing rock vibrated around them. One thrust of movement tossed Fergal to the ground and she fell beside the crystal. Bunyip, on his belly next to her, dragged the sword close between them.

They both stared as a small root grew from beneath the green crystal. A single leaf unfurled, sweeping the crystal onto its surface. Moving toward Fergal, the leaf placed the crystal into her paw. She took the sword from Bunyip, slid it next to her and dropped the crystal into the opening at the crux of the hilt. A flash of white light filled the cavern and a paw reached out and took hold of the sword. It was Waylond. He was on his feet, and he stared down at his two young friends. "Run, Fergal. Take Bunyip and run."

"But what about you, Waylond? I can't leave without you!" Fergal said.

"Yes, you can, and you will listen to me this one last time."

Bunyip took Fergal by the paw and pulled her toward the tunnel. "Come on, Fergal. It's time to go!"

Fergal gazed at Waylond, the numbat who saved her from the Gabbling, the companion that revealed himself to her, the friend she had come to understand and love. He smiled back at her, his eyes filled with tenderness, and she could see that he was serene in his purpose.

"I love you!" Fergal's final words echoed as Bunyip pulled her down the dark tunnel.

Chapter 27

Nedra emerged from the crevice in the mountain's base. She led the group of women and their children toward the safety of the Forest. The woods had blossomed, and the underbrush was thick, which would provide cover for the animals and the little ones. As they filed by her, Nedra squinted beneath the bright rays of the setting sun, a sun she had not seen in years. She glanced nervously around her, unsure of what to do or where to go. A paw gripped hers. When she looked down, Mirindah was looking up at her with a smile.

"It's okay, Nedra. We're out of the mountain. But we need to get everyone to the safety of the Forest."

"Of course," Nedra said. "Where do we go?"

"We'll head that way," Mirindah instructed. "We'll stay low and off any main paths, and we'll need to try to keep the babes quiet, just in case there are any more lizards and devils about." She glanced over her shoulder up at the mountain. One explosion after another rocked the earth, terrifying the little ones, who were crying and whining in fear.

A small dibbler with a crying babe in her arms stepped out of the group. "What about the menfolk?" she asked.

Nedra's concern for the women and children helped her to gather strength. "The Guardian promised that he would free them," Nedra said. She placed a paw on the woman's shoulder, and she saw faith shining in her eyes. The child in her arms thrust a paw into his mouth and began to suck contentedly. "It will be all right now. We will be all right now. We must believe in him. In any case, no one is going back in there." Nedra tilted her head toward the mountain.

When the group was within the safety of the Forest's foliage, Nedra took a moment to look around. Even though the erupting mountain threatened to destroy everything around her, and even though the black smoke billowing from its peak was now blocking the setting sun, she was still amazed by the world outside the caverns. It was a world that was barely a part of her memory, but she tried to recall it.

Her father's face came to her mind, briefly. It was like a shadow in the night and she could not hold the vision. This world had been taken from her, but that didn't matter anymore. Now she would revel in this new place; she would be different than she was before. She removed the remaining jewels she had at her wrists and tossed them into the greenery. There was no further need for them. She glanced at the opening at the base of Mt. Olga.

From the opening came a ragged group of men and boys. One of the little ones shouted, "Look! Here comes Papa!" He was jumping up and down and screaming with joy. Nedra had to hold him back.

"It's my Papa!" he yelled again.

"The men have been freed," cried one of the women.

Young critters jumped with joy as one by one they were reunited with their families.

Over the noise of the excited reunion, Nedra was sure she heard cries coming from the tunnel. She started walking back toward the opening when a paw took hold of her arm.

"You can't go back in there, Lady," a little grey dibbler said.

"I'll be right back," Nedra said. "Take everyone into the Forest and hide yourselves."

"No, we'll wait right here for you," the dibbler said. "You're one of us now."

"I'll be back as quickly as I can," Nedra said, smiling. "If I'm not back soon, hide!"

"Well, then," said the dibber, "you'd best hurry."

Nedra turned and walked back into the dark tunnel. She hadn't walked far when she saw something she had missed on her way out with the women and children. A screen of tightly woven roots had grown across the entrance to a side tunnel. Behind the roots, the face of a dragon lizard appeared, and a small scream escaped her lips. "Get us outta here!" one of them growled at her. Looking closely, she could make out a troop of lizards behind him.

Dragon lizards, she thought, *and devils. Why should I free them?* She started to back away when a voice boomed from behind her, "Move out of the way, Nedra." It was Bede carrying a staff. "What's happening here?" he said.

"They're stuck behind there," Nedra said.

Bede peered in at the lizards. He hesitated, then wedged the staff between the roots and began to pry them open as best he could. As he shoved and pushed, the staff began to glow, and the roots shriveled back, forming an opening. Bede stood back, staring down at the staff in his paw, and the lizards passing through the opening stared as well. The lead dragon lizard looked at Nedra and Bede, sizing up the situation. "I should take you both into custody and bring you back to Morlund."

Bede stepped in between the lizard and Nedra. Placing the staff firmly into the dirt, Bede said, "That would not be wise." Lifting the staff from the ground it began glowing again. The lizard's eyes widened with fright and amazement. After a slight gesture of his paw, his troops began filing out of the tunnel. The leader followed soon after, but not before turning to Bede. "I was wrong," he said, "and we thank you." With a nod he turned and ran.

"We've got to get out of here," Bede said, but movement from inside the mountain caught his attention. Flitch came into view, his tongue lolling out of the side of his mouth.

"What are you doing, Nedra?" he said with a growl.

Nedra took a step, placing herself right in front of Flitch. With a deep breath, she pulled her arm back, and punched the miserable dog in the snout. He staggered and sat back on his haunches, rubbing his muzzle. "That's what I'm doing, Flitch. Now get lost before I do it again!"

With a sneer, Flitch backed away and ran out of the tunnel disappearing into the woods.

Bede smiled up at Nedra. "Our work here is done," he said with a smile. "It's time to go."

"Bede! I'm so glad to see you." Rufus stepped out of the bushes as Bede came near. He slapped Bede on the shoulder playfully. "You told me this day would come."

"Yes, indeed, Rufus," Bede said. "Let's hope we see another." He narrowed his eyes and watched as flames and smoke erupted from the mountaintop.

Then Bede heard a familiar voice. "Bede, is that you?" Turning, he saw his mother move out from beneath a fern.

"Mother!" Bede dropped the staff and wrapped her in his arms.

"I can't believe it. It's over!" she said, wiping a tear from her snout.

Rufus held his hand out to Bede's mother. "Hello, I'm Rufus," he said. "Your son took care of my foot. I would not be walking if it weren't for Bede."

She took his paw and pulled him to her, engulfing him in a motherly hug. "I'm so glad to meet you, Rufus," she said, still hugging him. "My Bede has always been a good boy. That he has."

Bede chuckled a bit. "Come quickly, we must move farther away from the mountain. I don't think it's going to hold together much longer."

"Yes," agreed Nedra as she walked up from behind them.

"I never thought I would see you among us," Bede said. "I'm glad you're here." He gathered up the wooden staff and gazed up at Nedra.

"It seems there is always time for change," Nedra said. "Besides, it is good to feel the fresh air through my fur." She held her paws out. "Perhaps when this has all passed away, we can become friends."

"Perhaps," Bede replied. "For now, Rufus is right, we must move." The earth rattled again with a powerful jolt. Bede and Nedra hustled the group into the thick foliage. When he was certain that everyone was safe, he looked back. Mt. Olga was erupting in flames. Rocks and dirt slid down its side and ash began to shower down from above. Then two small creatures appeared at the mountain's base.

It was Fergal and Bunyip.

"Run, Fergal!" Nedra shouted.

Bunyip and Fergal streaked for the safety of the Forest, dashing between falling rocks.

Reaching Nedra's side, Fergal panted, taking in deep breaths again and again, she could barely speak. "Waylond!" she cried. "He's still in there." She began moving back toward the crevice, but it was now a small slit that even she would not be able to squeeze through.

Nedra wrapped her arms around Fergal. "It's all right, little one," she said. "He knew what he was doing all along."

Bunyip moved closer and stroked Fergal's head and rubbed her back, then pulled her close. Together they stared up at the erupting mountain.

Behind Nedra, the Forest's foliage separated and there stood Wulfgar, with one foot lifted slightly off the ground. Simkin held him up as best he could. The two were bent over, and it looked like Simkin might collapse at any second. Nedra moved in to lend a paw. Releasing Simkin from the weight of the injured stoat, she placed an arm beneath Wulfgar's and eased him to the ground.

"Simkin!" Bede ran to meet his brother, with his mother close behind. "Oh, Simkin," Bede said, embracing him. The two bilbies cried together as their mother, with tears welling up in her eyes, looked on with love and pride.

"I'm so glad that the families have been reunited," Nedra said.

Wulfgar looked at Nedra. "Is that what it's all about?" he asked, a sour look on his face. He rubbed his swollen leg and shook his head.

"Wulfgar!" The sound of Bunyip's voice made Wulfgar look up.

"Bunyip!" Wulfgar shouted. "Get over here, ya dang turnip of a stoat. Ya never listen to me. When I tells ya to stay put, I mean it. Ya should a never gone…that river should have never…" Wulfgar stopped short. Nedra looked down at him and then at Bunyip.

"Who is this stoat to you, Bunyip?"

"He's nobody, Nedra, nobody." Bunyip scrunched his nose and looked away.

"That's not true, my boy," Wulfgar said. "Not true. I – I…"

Wulfgar was sputtering. He rubbed his ears and fiddled nervously with the hilt of his dagger. Then he picked at the gold buttons on his vest and looked at everyone who stood before him.

"I'm not 'nobody,' my boy," Wulfgar said, glancing up at Bunyip. "I'm yer Uncle."

"My what!" Bunyip exclaimed, turning back to confront Wulfgar.

"Hard to believe, ain't it?" Wulfgar said. "Come here, boy!" Wulfgar stopped and shook his head. He held out a paw to Bunyip. "Please, boy, come here. I am truly sorry for keeping this from ya, but it was difficult, ya see, with all the men…and me bein' in charge and all…"

Bunyip took a step toward Wulfgar, then stopped.

"Go ahead, Bunyip," Fergal said. "You have family."

"You're my family, Fergal," Bunyip said.

"Yes, that's true, and that will never change, but Wulfgar's your uncle. You can't change that either. Just like my brothers," she laughed. "You can't change relations. They'll always be yours, for good or bad." She laughed again and Wulfgar joined in.

"So true," Wulfgar said. He leaned out and took Bunyip's paw in his. "Can ya forgive this mean old curmudgeon of a stoat?"

A huge fireball exploded from the top of the mountain.

"Everyone get down!" Nedra shouted.

A blast of sparks shot from the peak and filled the air above their heads. Nedra reached out and drew Fergal against her. She saw Bunyip and his uncle huddling together. By their side was Bede with his brother and mother. *At least we're all together*, she thought.

Chapter 28

I love you too, Fergal, Waylond thought. He gripped the sword in his paw and strode toward his bother, who continued to struggle against the roots that held him to the rock wall. His paws were balled into fists, and he pulled and tugged, the strain of it clear on his contorted face. Waylond placed the point of his sword at his brother's throat.

"What? Will you kill me now, brother?" Morlund spat at Waylond. "Is that what the Guardian would do?"

Morlund's words made Waylond stop. He held the sword tightly in his paw, as he looked deep into his brother's eyes. "Morlund, there's no need for this."

"Kill me, brother, or free me," Morlund said. "I'll never stop fighting you."

"But why, Morlund?"

"Don't you realize what you did? Everything is gone. Mother…"

"That was an accident, Morlund. It wasn't your fault."

"No! It was *your* fault," Morlund wailed. "You stood by and did nothing."

"I tried! I was young...a mere child, untested."

"You didn't try hard enough, Waylond. You had powers, but you didn't try hard enough. You were not worthy to be the Guardian. You weren't then and you're not worthy now."

"I was a child. Don't you think I would have done anything I could?"

"I'm tired of hearing this. Go ahead, kill me and prove your worth!"

With a grin, Waylond said, "You're right, Morlund. I need to prove my worth, and indeed I will. Remember, Morlund, the power of the sword is not mine alone," he said. "It is given freely by the Forest, and the Forest will continue as it always has." With those last words Waylond raised the sword above his head. Morlund closed his eyes.

Waylond swept the sword down, swinging it in a circle, missing Morlund entirely. As the sword pointed upward in its arc, Waylond roared, and releasing his grip on the weapon, the blade streaked skyward through the peak of the mountain. The mountaintop exploded and the powerful force sent the sword soaring across the sky like a shooting star, a trail of green light in its wake.

"Why did you do that?" shouted Morlund.

"The Guardian truly becomes one when he believes in himself, believes that he is worthy to be the Guardian."

Waylond saw the realization in Morlund's face. "But I am *worthy*!" he yelled. "I am *worthy*!"

"You know that's not true, Morlund, and it never will be because you don't really believe it." Waylond took a step closer to his brother. With a wave of his paw, the roots released Morlund and he fell to the ground. "I release you, Morlund. Now if only you can do the same for yourself." With that, Waylond held out a paw to his brother.

Morlund sank to his knees and began to sob. Waylond stood for a moment in silence, mourning all that had been lost and all that he had gained from his journey. He gripped his brother's shoulders and lifted him and embraced him. Then tilting his head back he looked up through the opening in the mountain to the now darkening sky where the stars were beginning to come out, sparkling one by one. He knew that he was now ready to be the Guardian. He could feel the love of his mother and father, and in a burst of light, he, along with his brother, became one with them. The room was filled with a golden glow, and when it faded away, Waylond and his brother were no more.

Chapter 29

Sparks filled the sky—twisting and drifting down like flaming snowflakes. The darkening heavens became streaked with brilliant red, yellow, and orange. The sheer beauty of it was hard to contemplate as red-hot rocks shot through the trees, crashing through branches, lighting brush on fire, and falling all around them with immense force. There was nowhere to run. They were all going to burn.

Simkin was about to put his claws into his mouth when he felt a tug on his vest. A young wide-eyed dibbler with tears streaming down his face stood at his feet. "I've lost my papa," he cried pitifully.

Simkin pulled his paw away from his mouth and quickly drew the youngster against him.

"Right now, I'm your papa, child," Simkin said. He clutched the babe to him, lay down on the ground, and covered the child with his body. Both lay still waiting for the inevitable.

It seemed that a long time had gone by. *The flaming boulders should have hit us by now*, Simkin thought. With the child tucked safely under him, he mustered all his courage, slowly opened his eyes, and looked up. The trees above were forming a net. The leaves and the branches were knitting a blanket of green overhead. All around, the Forest was shielding the ground and the creatures that were clustered together there. No sparks or falling debris penetrated the thick web. The sound of the stones hitting the leaves and branches could be heard, and the hissing of the sparks being extinguished by the foliage was music to Simkin's long ears. He jumped to his feet with the dibbler babe held tightly to his chest. "Look, everyone!" he shouted. "The Forest has protected us." The dibbler in his arms wiped a tear that had escaped from Simkin's eye. The child patted Simkin's snout.

"It's the Guardian!" the youngster said. "His power is protecting us."

"Yes, I'm sure you're right," Simkin said.

"Tarka! I'm so glad your safe." An adult dibbler ran toward Simkin, a smile bursting across his snout.

"Papa," the young dibbler cried. He held out his arms and was whisked into his father's.

"Thank you for taking care of him," the dibbler said to Simkin.

"It was nothing," Simkin responded.

"No, sir, it was everything." The dibbler hugged the babe and began to walk away. He stopped, glanced over his shoulder one last time and said, "Thank you for your kindness and your courage."

Simkin could only nod. He was stunned, and his whole being felt different. He couldn't quite put his claw on it, but he felt taller, stronger. He felt like he could make a difference. He cleared his throat and was about to bring a claw up to bite. He stopped in mid-movement and looked at his claws. "Hmm," he said. "They don't need a clipping."

His brother came up from behind. "No, Simkin," Bede said as he slapped his brother on the back, "they certainly do not!"

They chuckled together for a moment, when suddenly the earth moved beneath their feet.

"Oh no, not again," Nedra said.

Bede and Simkin stared at her. Then all three gazed at the peak of Mt. Olga. Soon the entire group stood staring. White smoke was now pouring out the top of the mountain. It formed clouds of mist that floated away. A streak of mist the color of the Forest flew across the sky leaving a trail of green light behind it.

"I wonder what that was," Bede said as he gazed up.

"Get back everyone!" Simkin shouted. "Hide beneath the underbrush and stay there. Don't move." Every dibbler, quokka, quoll, and bilby scurried away and disappeared from sight, leaving Nedra, Bede and Simkin standing alone with Fergal and Bunyip nearby. They watched as a cloud of white descended over their heads. It formed itself into the image of wings, which then grew into a magnificent white owl. The owl was bigger than any that Simkin had ever seen. He spread his wings and continued to float serenely down. Extending his massive talons, the owl settled on the branch of a nearby gum tree, which bent under his weight.

"What's happening?" Nedra asked. "I think I hear someone whispering."

"I'm not sure," Simkin replied, "It sounds like it's coming from the trees."

They watched in awe at the bird high above them in the trees. His round, yellow eyes glowed, and he gazed down at the creatures gathered at the base of the ghost gum. The bird spread his wings, and his white feathers glistened in the starlight that now filled a glorious night sky.

Bede stepped forward with Waylond's staff clasped in his paw.

"Who are you?" he asked the owl.

The owl made no reply, but simply flapped his wings. His head swiveled and Simkin followed his stare. His gaze came to rest on Fergal and Bunyip.

"Maybe he wants us to do something," Fergal said.

"Yeah, but what?" Bunyip asked.

The owl then moved his head to look at Simkin. "Come over here," Simkin said. Fergal took Bunyip's paw and together they walked over to where Simkin, Nedra and Bede stood. When all five came together the owl looked down.

"If I didn't know any better," Bede said. "I'd swear he was smiling at..."

Before Bede could finish his sentence, the owl let out a haunting sound. It filled the Forest, and the leaves on all the trees quivered and shook in response. It was then that the Verdigris spoke.

"We have taken Waylond with us," the voices began. "He will stand beside his father, taking his place as Guardian of the Forest. All uncertainty, negative thoughts, and feelings have left him. He will watch over you now, but you must promise to watch over each other." A hush fell over the Forest as the voice of Guardians past spoke, and a warm breeze ruffled the fur on each and every creature gathered there. It seemed as though the Forest was extending itself to touch them. "Waylond is a friend to all of you, bilbies, dibblers, kowaries, quolls, quokkas and wallabies. He will care for the birds, lizards, stoats and devils. Everyone will be protected.

"What happened here should never happen again. Take care of one another, and guard each other as Waylond guards you. Oswin, the owl, will be his eyes in the Forest. The Styx will no longer be an island within the realm. It will now join the entire Forest and will be a part of it from this day forward. You can now cross into the Styx without fear, and it will grow and become one with the Forest." Oswin hooted from his perch in the gum tree. "Take nothing more from the Forest than you need, and give back to the Forest and your fellow creatures when you can." The voices of the Guardians faded, leaving Oswin the owl on the ghost gum. With little effort, the powerful bird launched himself from the branch and disappeared into the sky.

Epilogue

Bright sunlight danced on the waters of the billabong, and a light breeze blew the reeds that grew close to the banks. A shadow passed overhead and Oswin the owl landed on the branch of a nearby tingle tree. He shook his feathered wings, and brought a claw up to scratch the side of his head. Round eyes, set in a heart shaped face, scanned the countryside. He watched every creature that scurried across the long stretch of green lawn leading up to the foundation that was taking shape at the base of the thickly forested hill. Debris was being taken away from the building site in wheelbarrows, while freshly carved blocks of stone were arriving from the nearby granite quarry. Fergal and Bede were seated on a curved stone bench near the water's edge. A teapot and bowl of berries sat between them. They watched the bustle of the creatures hurrying by.

Oswin announced his arrival to the workers with a loud hoot.

Fergal looked up. "Oh, Oswin!" she said. "When did you get here?"

Oswin simply stared back, a serene look on his face.

Bede chuckled and set a paw on Fergal's shoulder. "He's taking notes!" Bede said. "He'll be reporting back to Waylond soon enough."

Fergal nodded in agreement. "Ah, yes, I'm sure you're right."

"No, no, no," a frustrated voice echoed nearby. "I don't want that there. Bring it over there, on the right side of the foundation! That's where it goes."

"Simkin!" Bede shouted at his brother. "Come, take a break with us. Fergal and I were about to share a pot of mint tea, berries, and nuts."

Simkin strode down the expanse of lawn toward Fergal and Bede with a small hammer in his paw.

"Well, how goes it, Simkin?" Fergal asked.

"It's not easy. No, not at all." He let out a long sigh and plopped his rear on the ground. His front legs extended before him and his belly flopped over his belt. "Lots more work to be done, but it's coming along." He touched his full stomach and said, "Please tell Mama to stop baking those rhubarb pies."

Bede chuckled. "You might as well ask night not to follow day."

A bright red ball rolled toward them and hit Simkin's back. Startled, he saw six young kowaries running to catch it. Simkin scooped the ball up. "Here ya go, young ones," he said, as he threw the ball up the bank. Bede, Fergal and Simkin watched as the children ran away after it.

"They are certainly thriving here," Bede said. He studied Fergal, lifted the teapot and poured another cup for her. "Would you like some?" he asked Simkin.

"Oh, I would love to sit and chat, but there is so much more to do." Simkin pointed to the construction site. "The abbey needs reinforcing on that right side, where we have planned the library, and the stained glass window is coming along splendidly. Nedra is helping the craftsmen build it. She's enjoying learning a new skill." He picked a red raspberry from the bowl on the bench, and swallowed it. "Mmm, very good berry crop."

"Yes, those berries are delicious. Mother's gardening abilities have been put to good use," Bede said. "And as for Nedra, it's so good to see her happy and doing something she truly enjoys."

"I agree with that," Fergal added. "The window is going to be beautiful. And your mother's berry crop is a plus. My stomach thanks your mother!"

"We've made great progress on the tower." Simkin nodded in the direction of a half raised stone edifice that climbed toward the trees. "We'll be able to keep a lookout from up there. The realm is peaceful now, but one never knows."

"Oh, look who's coming." Fergal pointed toward two stoats walking toward them. They were nose to nose, talking excitedly.

"Every child likes a bunk bed," Fergal heard one say, "and we'll be able to accommodate more in the dormitory if we stack them in threes." Wulfgar's voice carried down to the billabong, as did his nephew's.

"Uncle Wulfgar, they won't be safe up there on the top." Bunyip's face was filled with concern, and his brow was wrinkled in thought. "I'm not comfortable with that."

"They're young men, ya know," Wulfgar growled. "If they fall, they'll get up. A little spill off a bunk never hurt anyone. I'll be givin' those young ones some sword lessons as well."

Bunyip groaned. "Some things never change," he said. "Isn't that right, Fergal? What do you think about bunks stacked three high?"

Fergal turned to Bede. His word on the building of the abbey was final, and he made the major decisions and settled any arguments.

Raising an eyebrow, he said, "Well, we certainly need to give that consideration. Safety of the children is an utmost concern. I think we should also discuss your plan to put swords in the paws of little ones," he said, looking at Wulfgar.

"Yes, yes, we can discuss it." Wulfgar mumbled. "Did you know that my nephew here is a whiz with a hammer and nails? He's a fine carpenter, just like his father was." Wulfgar smiled proudly down at his nephew. "Let's get back to work, Bunyip. We'll talk some more as we go." Wulfgar wrapped an arm around Bunyip, who smiled up at his uncle.

"We'll figure it out, Bede," Bunyip said over his shoulder at the bilby. "No worries."

"I have no doubt about that," Bede said. He was smiling ear to ear.

Fergal had never seen him so content since his decision to build the abbey. It would be called Acadia Abbey, and it would be a shelter for all lost or abandoned creatures of the surrounding lands of Sunderland. Building the abbey had everyone who had escaped Mt. Olga smiling and lending a paw in one way or another. Although they had not seen him since that fateful day, they felt the Guardian's presence and guiding paw in all that they did.

"Lunch break is over," Simkin said, getting to his feet. "Rufus is cutting more blocks for the foundation on the south side of the building, and I have to make sure he has help moving the ones he's already cut safely to the site."

"Sounds good," Bede said with a nod. "We need to get a move on as well." Bede watched as his brother head across the lawn toward the forge.

Fergal grabbed the teapot and bowl of berries and the two headed up the lawn together.

"What has Nedra designed for the stained glass window, Bede?" Fergal asked.

"I'm not exactly sure, but I believe she said something about the sword. You remember, the one with that green crystal in its hilt."

"Of course I remember," she said. "I helped Waylond bring it all the way to Mt. Olga." She became silent and stopped in her tracks.

"What is it, Fergal?" Bede asked. "What's bothering you, dear?"

"Oh, I don't know, Bede," she said in a reflective tone. "I guess I miss Waylond."

"I'm sure you do, but Waylond knew he had to accept his responsibility. The Forest called to him and he had to answer. He is one with her now." He placed his paw gently on her cheek. "We love you, Fergal. We're your family here, but I am sure that he watches over you every day. After all, he was the first family you found after you were washed away from your own by the Gabbling."

"Yes, you're right, Bede," Fergal said, as she began walking again. "I did love him so, and who knows, maybe someday I'll find my way back to my home near the Gabbling!"

"Now that's the spirit!" Bede's smile made Fergal feel warm inside. The love he radiated felt almost the same as Waylond's.

"What do you think has happened to that sword?" Fergal asked.

"I have no idea," Bede said. "But I'm sure it's safe in Waylond's paws." He smiled at her, and his eyes shone with the same love and kindness she had known with Waylond. It warmed her. At that moment she knew that the journey had been worth the walk.

The End

Bede, Fergal, and Simkin, by the Billabong

GLOSSARY

Arum Lily

The Arum Lily is a beautiful white flower with a central yellow spike. It blooms in many Australian gardens. Both the flower and the sap are considered poisonous. The sap can cause a terrible rash and the flowers are exceptionally toxic. (Photo Credit: Author, via Shutterstock)

Australian Masked Owl (AKA – Barn Owl)

The Australian Masked Owl is closely related to, and looks very much like a barn owl. It is listed as 'least concern' on the International Union for Conservation of Nature and Natural Resources (IUCN) list and can be found in much of the non-desert areas of Australia. I have taken the liberty in our story, to make Oswin completely white. To learn more about the Australian Masked Owl, and to hear the sound it makes, click on the following link and click where it says 'typical call, female:www.owlpages.com/owls.php?genus=Tyto&species=no vaehollandiae

(Photo credit: Richard Jackson)

Bilby

The bilby is a desert-dwelling marsupial (see below) found in Australia. At one time, there were two species, but one became extinct in the 1950s. The term bilby comes from an Aboriginal word meaning long-nosed rat. It is sometimes referred to by the nickname, pinkie. It is listed as 'vulnerable' by the IUCN. To learn more about the bilby, visit this site:

www.arkive.org/greater-bilby/macrotis-lagotis/

(Image Credit: Author, via Shutterstock)

Billabong

A Billabong is a small lake, usually located adjacent to a river. The water in a billabong is typically still.

(Photo Credit: Author, via Shutterstock)

Boab Tree

The boab tree grows in Africa, Madagascar and Australia. It is easily recognizable by its swollen trunk and stems. These stems contain large amounts of water, which enable the tree to deal with seasonal droughts. To learn more about the boab, visit this site:

www.bbc.co.uk/nature/life/Adansonia#p00f815d

(Photo credit: www.kimberlyaustralia.com)

Brown Snake

The Brown Snake, also known as the king brown snake, can be found all along the east coast of Australia. Even the venom of a baby brown snake can kill a human. This snake is responsible for most snakebite deaths in Australia. To learn more about the brown snake, visit this site:

www.arkive.org/king-brown-snake/pseudechis-australis/

(Photo credit: Author's own collection)

Dibbler

The dibbler is one of the most rare and endangered marsupials in the world. It lives on two small islands off the southwest coast of Australia. This tiny mouse-like carnivore is busy at dawn and dusk when it hunts small insects, lizards and even birds. To learn more about the dibbler, go to this site: www.arkive.org/dibbler/parantechinus-apicalis/

(Image Credit: Amy (Kit) Prendergast)

Dragon Lizard (Gippsland Water Dragon)

This lizard is also known as the Australian Water Dragon. It is an arboreal (lives in the trees) species of lizard. They have long powerful limbs for climbing and a strong tail for swimming. This Australian lizard is quite common and therefore not endangered. To learn more about the water dragon lizard, visit this site:

www.en.wikipedia.org/wiki/Australian_water_dragon

(Photo Credit: Ian Jardine-Queensland, Australia)

Ghost Gum (Gum Tree – see also Tingle Tree)

Gum Tree is a general term that covers a number of different species of tree, including Eucalyptus trees, which Koala's love to eat. Most Gum Trees are found in Australia, but there are also some, which occur outside the country. The Ghost Gum has an unusually white and smooth bark. It is especially beautiful on a moonlit night. To learn more about gum trees, visit this site:

www.australia.gov.au/about-australia/australian-story/eucalypts

(Photo Credit: Author, via Shutterstock)

Gympie-Gympie

The gympie-gympie grows in the tropical rainforests of Australia. It is extremely toxic. Even the dead leaves of the plant can cause a painful sting that has been compared to an attack by multiple wasps. The pain can reoccur over a period of months. To learn more about the gympie-gympie, visit this site:

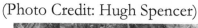

www.australiangeographic.com.au/topics/science-environment/2014/02/factsheet-gympie-gympie

(Photo Credit: Hugh Spencer)

Laughing Kookaburra

The Kookaburra is known worldwide by school children thanks to the wonderful song about the kookaburra sitting in the old gum tree. Fortunately, the kookaburra is not endangered and is found widely across Australia. To learn more about the kookaburra, visit this site:

www.en.wikipedia.org/wiki/Kookaburra

(Photo Credit: From the author's own collection.)

Platypus

The Platypus is a very unusual animal. It has a bill like a duck, a tail like a beaver, and webbed feet like an otter. It is a monotreme (definition below). Besides laying eggs, and nursing their babies via a 'milk patch,' this unusual mammal also has a poisonous spike or spur on its rear ankle. This venomous spike is found only on the males and it is used against predators and other male platypuses. The platypus is not endangered. To learn more about the platypus, visit this site:

www.arkive.org/platypus/ornithorhynchus-anatinus/
(Photo Credit: Author, via Shutterstock)

Kowari

The Kowari is also known as the brush-tailed marsupial rat. That alone says a lot about the appearance of this little creature. It is a carnivorous animal that lives in the dry grasslands and deserts of central Australia. It is listed as 'vulnerable' on the IUCN list. To learn more about the kowari, visit this site: www.arkive.org/kowari/dasyuroides-byrnei/image-G36647.html)

(Photo Credit: Vladimir Motycka – Arkive.org © **Vladimír Motycka**

Marsupial

A marsupial is a kind of mammal that has a pouch. Their babies are born in a very immature state and mature inside their mothers pouches attached to her nipples. The babies will stay inside their mother's pouch for weeks or months, depending on the species. Some digging marsupials like the quoll, for example, have their pouches on backwards so that when the mothers dig they do not get dirt in their pouch. To learn more about marsupials, visit this site:

www.ucmp.berkeley.edu/mammal/marsupial/marsupial.html

Monotreme

A monotreme is the most primitive mammal. There are only two monotremes on the planet, the echidna and the platypus. These two mammals lay eggs. Once the babies hatch the mother nurses them with milk on a 'milk patch'. Monotremes do not have teats like normal mammals. To learn more about monotremes, visit this site:

www.ucmp.berkeley.edu/mammal/monotreme.html

Mt. Olga

Mount Olga, which is known as Kata Tjuta (Kata Joota) by the Aborigines is actually a group of rocks in the center of Australia. It shares geological space with Ayers Rock, or Uluru, as the Aborigines know it. There are a total of thirty-six rocks that make up the Olgas, the highest being almost 3,500 feet above sea level. To learn more about Kata Tjuta, visit this site:

www.en.wikipedia.org/wiki/Kata_Tjuta

(Photo Credit: From the author's own collection)

Numbat

The Numbat is a small colorful marsupial, which is also known as the banded anteater. It has a finely pointed nose and a bushy tail. Once upon a time, it could be found across the southern regions of Australia. However, now its range is restricted and it is considered 'endangered' on the IUCN list. To learn more about numbats, go to this site:

www.arkive.org/numbat/myrmecobius-fasciatus/

(Photo Credit: Amy (Kit) Prendergast)

Quoll

There are several species of this small marsupial. The Quoll is carnivorous and will eat small mammals, birds, lizards and insects. Its numbers have declined since Australia was colonized, and one species has become extinct. The Northern Quoll is being repopulated to an island in an effort to protect it. Urban development and poison baiting are major threats to the Quoll. Depending on the species, they are listed as 'threatened' and 'endangered' on the IUCN. To learn more about the Quoll, go to this site:

www.arive.org/eastern-quoll/dayurusviverrinus

(Photo credit: Author's own collection)

Quokka

The Quokka is a marsupial that is about the size of a domestic cat. It is nocturnal (comes out at night), and it is herbivorous (eats plants). Although it was once thought to be extinct, a population was found on Rottnest Island off Perth, in Western Australia. Other small populations have been located on the mainland. It was one of the first animals seen by the Europeans who first set foot on the shores of Australia and is considered 'vulnerable' on the IUCN list. To learn more about the Quokka, go to this site:

www.arkive.org/quokka/setonixbrachyurus

(Photo Credit: Wikimedia-Quokka-Raffi Kojian-CIMG6317)

Southern Cassowary

The southern cassowary is a large flightless bird that is found in the tropical rainforests of New Guinea, Indonesia and northeastern Australia. It has a hard crown on its head, which it uses to push through thick vegetation in the rainforests. It also has a dagger-like claw, on each foot. It uses a powerful kick to protect itself from predators. To learn more about the southern cassowary, visit this site:

www.arkive.org/southern-cassowary/casuarius-casuarius/

(Image Credit: Wikimedia – public domain)

Stoat

Stoats are carnivorous mammals and a member of the weasel family. They have long slender bodies that are typically reddish or ginger colored with a cream underside. The stoat is not indigenous to Australia, but I took the liberty of using this animal in our story. They are typically found in northern climates such as, North American, Europe, Asia and even Greenland. To learn more about stoats, visit this site:

www.arkive.org/stoat/mustela-erminea/

(Photo Credit: Author, via Shutterstock)

Tasmanian Devil

Like the wallaby and the kangaroo, the Tasmanian devil is a marsupial so it does have a pouch. However, the pouch is turned backwards like many other digging marsupials. The devil is credited with a haunting screech that can be heard during the night. It lives in Tasmania. To learn more about the Tasmanian Devil, visit this site:

www.arkive.org/tasmanian-devil/sarcophilus-harrisii/

(Photo Credit: Amy (Kit) Prendergast)

Thylacine

The Thylacine was a very interesting animal. Unfortunately, we can only see them in pictures because they are extinct. The last living thylacine was seen in the 1950s in Tasmania, which is an island off the coast of southeastern Australia. This mammal was considered a wolf marsupial, a very strange combination indeed! It appeared to be a cross between a wolf and a tiger, but it also had a pouch in which its offspring would grow. To learn more about the thylacine, go to this site:

www.arkive.org/thylacine/thylacinus-cynocephalus/

(Image Credit: Wikimedia – public domain)

Tingle Tree (see also Gum Tree)

The Tingle Tree is a species of eucalyptus, and is also known as a Gum Tree. There are many species of this type of tree. There is a giant tingle tree in Australia that is considered the oldest living eucalypt in the world. To learn more about Gum Trees, visit this site:

www.encyclopedia.com/topic/gum_tree.aspx

(Photo Credit: Author, via Shutterstock)

Wallaby

There are many different species of Wallaby, and they vary in terms of endangerment. They are like miniature Kangaroos and weigh thirty-five to forty pounds. Like Kangaroos, the Wallaby has a pouch in which their offspring grows. Also, like Kangaroos, the Wallaby baby is called a joey. To learn more about Wallabies, visit this site:

www.animals.nationalgeographic.com/animals/mammals/wallaby/

(Photo credit: Alex Meyer)

Wedge-Tailed Eagle

The Wedge-Tailed Eagle is Australia's largest bird of prey and also considered one of the world's largest eagles. It derives its name from its long, diamond shaped tail. To learn more about the Wedge-Tailed Eagle, visit this site:

www.arkive.org/wedge-tailed-eagle/aquila-audax/

(Photo Credit: From the author's own collection)

Windjana Gorge

Windjana Gorge is a national park located in Western Australia. The gorge was formed by the Lennard River, which flows during the wet season, but creates pools along its route during the dry season. To learn more about the gorge, visit this site:

www.kimberleyaustralia.com/windjana-gorge-national-park.html

(Photo Credit: Author, via Shutterstock)

Wombat

There are three main species of Wombat. The Northern Hairy-nosed Wombat is 'critically endangered' on the IUCN list. Two other species are of least concern. It is a short-legged marsupial that lives in burrow systems. It has powerful front claws and rodent-like teeth. Interesting fact: the Wombat's pouch is backwards so that it doesn't get dirt into it while digging. To learn more about wombats, visit: www.arkive.org/southern-hairy-nosed-wombat/lasiorhinus-latifrons/

(Photo Credit: Author, via Shutterstock)

ABOUT THE AUTHOR

J.E. Rogers is a graduate of Western Connecticut State University. Infused with a reverence for life, she loves animals and has always been especially intrigued by the unusual wildlife that can only be found in Australia. An avid student of every facet of the country, Rogers' love of all things Australian has flowed into her books. She hopes to spark an interest in young readers to the flora and fauna of the Land Down Under, while engaging them in a wildly imaginative tale of adventure.

She spends much of her time blogging and speaking to youngsters, at libraries, schools, and museums, about endangered and threatened animals around the globe. She wants children to understand that we are connected with all life on this planet, that animals are our fellow creatures and we share this world with them. It is our responsibility to protect them.

Jeanne lives in Connecticut with her family, which includes two dogs, and two cats.

58553695R00137

Made in the USA
Charleston, SC
13 July 2016